With the exception of the professional sports and entertainment figures and colleges, all characters mentioned in this book are fictitious. Any similarities to persons, places or things are purely coincidental.

DAVID ELYDGE VENCIL

WHAT YOU GONNA DO WHEN YOU GET THERE?

Written and illustrated by
Daud Nnamdi
COPR. MCMXCVIII

AuthorHouse™
1663 Liberty Drive, Suite 200
Bloomington, IN 47403
www.authorhouse.com
Phone: 1-800-839-8640

First published by AuthorHouse   6/18/2008

ISBN: 978-1-4343-8847-6 (sc)

Printed in the United States of America
Bloomington, Indiana

This book is printed on acid-free paper.

authorHOUSE®

ACKNOWLEDGEMENTS

Inspiration is the bedrock of any endeavor. In saying this, I must let the world and you readers know that my bedrock is God the Father, Son and Holy Ghost; He who gave me life and the most precious of all gifts, my wife, Dorothea Rochelle Vencil. "An excellent wife is the crown her husband…" (Proverbs 12:4). Her laughter is infectious and her counsel, invaluable. In a word, she is LOVE. Next are 3BK, our three sons, Kevin, Kamil and Karim; our future and present joy.

Special thanks to Chandra Cheesborough for allowing me to use her position, Women's Track and Field Coach, to establish the criteria which would qualify a young woman to be considered for a scholarship to the Tennessee State University track and field program – you are a true champion.

To my Uncle, Lloyd P., and Aunt Dolores B. Boucree; thank you for introducing me to the art of proofreading and your labor of love, spending precious hours editing this book. I love you as do Dot and the boys.

Eternal gratitude to my sisters, Connie, Maria, Gee Gee and La Dawn; whose laughter while proofreading the draft inspired me to make the book a reality.

And lastly, much love and thanks to my niece Tabitha (Nikki) and Miss Tiffani Wilder, outstanding track pupil, who by deeming this book "the bomb" validates its appeal to the teenager and young adult reader.

DEDICATION

In memory of my Nana, Juanita Calhoun Taylor, and her sister, Essie Thompson, my Godmother – to all the special women in my life, I pray they watch over each of you from heaven just as they did here on earth.

PREFACE

A small circle of friends are sitting in an airport lobby discussing their apprehension with leaving home for college and career. "…Girl, I don't know what I'm going to do without you guys in Colorado." "You know?! We've been together for a long time." "But this year has been the trip girl, starting with Homecoming…"

TABLE OF CONTENTS

MISS MARSHALL HIGH

"**Y**ou better recognize," the crowd chanted while waving their hands in the air and doing the Marshall Strut to the beat of FUNKY BIG BAND, the dance hit by Janet Jackson. It was Homecoming and Malcolm Tate had just scored again, increasing Marshall's lead to 21-3 over East Crenshaw. Four minutes left until half-time and the homecoming festivities. Sitting in the bleachers, always on the fourth row behind the 50 yard line, sat Micah and Nona Henderson, anxiously awaiting the coronation of Miss Marshall High. Their "Baby Girl", Chenelle, was practically guaranteed to wear that honor after tonight. Although the Henderson name had been associated with Marshall Football for the last 10 years, this was the first time a Henderson wasn't actually suited up and playing. Her three older brothers had been football standouts and until this year she'd been a cheerleader. Hearing the staccato TAT-TAT-TAT-TAT of the snare drums, followed by the thunderous bass drum roll, the Hendersons listened for the clash of the cymbals which would coincide with the ensuing kick-off. Kenyan, their youngest child, brandished these noisy instruments with both dread and pride, being a freshman member of the High Steppin' Marshall Panthers.

"Boom" went the bass and the football sailed through the air tumbling end over end. East Crenshaw's return specialist, Lavell Morris, looked up-field planning his route as his teammates began to form a wall on the right hash mark. Touted as the next Eric Metcalf or Deion Sanders, Lavell had the potential to "go all the way" at least once a game. Marshall's kick-off coverage team was the best in the conference and was determined to remain so. "He ain't all that," Eric (Foots) Prater encouraged his teammates before putting all he had into the oblong piece of leather now tumbling through the air. "Lavell Morris is on the Crenshaw two yard line. Will he make it 21-9?," the Marshall announcer asked mockingly. "Here we go…, here we go, here we go, here we go!," the Tiger fans began chanting as number #21 cut right toward his wall of blockers. "He's at the 10, cuts across field to the 15, up the left hash mark; he's at the 20!, he might do it people…!, the announcer warned with a mixture of concern and sarcasm. Those in the bleachers on the visitors' side of the field stood and began to wave the maize and black streamers as the Tiger cheerleaders and mascot led them in the cheer "S-C-O-R-E, SCORE-SCORE!" "Deion Sanders better watch out!," the announcer continued his harangue as Lavell spun away from Mason Cole, #91, who was attempting to wrap him up at the knees. "He cuts right at the 22, he's going…" Just as suddenly as Lavell turned up-field he felt himself being lifted off his feet and propelled backward. The air left his body as he hit the ground. Hearing what he thought to be a thunder clap, he opened his eyes to see Damon Edwards, #95, standing over him with his helmet raised in the air.

When Kenyan saw Mason Cole had Lavell in his grasp, he stood – anticipating the crushing hit soon to be delivered by Damon. Following his lead, the rest of the cymbal section stood ready to do a "ripple." When Lavell's feet came off the ground the cymbals clashed one after the other until the sound reverberated throughout the stadium. The Marshall band and student body stood, pointed across the field, and chided the East Crenshaw fans, "DON'T BELIEVE THE HYPE." Mason Cole pulled his helmet off as he ran over to congratulate Damon. He wore his hair pulled into a ponytail behind his head, yet cut close, just above the ears, extending to the nape of the neck. He and Damon were inseparable during football season; a salt and pepper tandem, Damon nicknamed "Demonseed" and Mason nicknamed "Spawn." "Way to stay at home fellas," Coach Hawk congratulated his two hellions when they reached the sidelines. The half would end with Damon being run down from behind after recovering a fumble, and then stripped of the ball at the four yard line by none other than Lavell Morris. Half-time score: 21-3.

The band played "Isn't She Lovely?" as the six beautiful young ladies were escorted from alternating end zones. Each was greeted with cheers, while a brief bio was read describing the unique qualities for which she'd been nominated for this esteemed honor. Each beamed radiantly, smiling at the crowd and trying to see their families through the glaring stadium lights. Each bubbled, relishing the feel of the violet carpet of mock roses crushing beneath her feet on her way to the stage majestically placed in the center of the field. "Ladies, gentlemen, alumni, and Marshall High students; please join me in singing the Marshall High Alma Mater, after which we will crown MISS MARSHALL HIGH 1994-95!," announced Mr. Marksbury, the principal, himself a 1965 graduate of the then segregated Bradford High. The stadium was abuzz throughout the last stanza of the alma mater as the questions, "who did you vote for?" and "who do you think won," were asked by students, parents, and alumni alike. "Pride, Equality, and Justice always and forever," the crowd finished singing. The trumpets announced the moment all were waiting for. "Will the parents of these beautiful young ladies please stand?," Mr. Marksbury began. "We, the faculty, alumni, and student body thank and commend you for the fine job you've done with your daughters, trusting us to fulfill our part of the contract to provide them with the tools and knowledge to be the women of tomorrow and the best at whatever endeavor they may choose for their future. While there will only be one queen crowned this evening, they are all winners. Once again, we applaud you and thank you for being part of the Marshall High family!" The crowd applauded.

"Nona, you're about to break my fingers, baby!," Micah sighed as she squeezed his hand anxiously. The chorus sang "Black Butterfly" by Sounds of Blackness. Upon the finish of Black Butterfly, the stadium was silent and still. Chenelle reached out to hold the hands of Monica Braxton and Amina Thompson on her right and left and they in turn reached out to the young ladies beside them. With the angelic timbre of the French horn in the background came the announcement, "Ladies and Gentlemen, I give you CHENELLE LATRICE HENDERSON, MISS MARSHALL HIGH 1994-95." Although Micah had promised Nona he'd behave if Chenelle won, he stood and shouted, pumping his fist into the air. Monica was first to graciously kiss Chenelle, then Amina and the three remaining nominees. Heike Graham, the seemingly only white nominee was last, giving her an encouraging "you go girl!" before leaving the stage. Chenelle was escorted off-stage to the music of Whitney Houston singing "I'm Every Woman." Marshall High went on to win 42-20. The band played "You Can't Touch This" as the bleachers began to empty and the players headed to their respective locker rooms.

Kadeem was a bright young man set on attending Howard University to major in Political Science. He had been part of the student government these last three years. Starting as class treasurer in his sophomore year, he rose to vice president as a junior, finally ascending to student council president, this his last and senior year at Marshall High. Tonight, however, Kadeem was both Chenelle's escort and date. He'd waited six years for this honor. Kadeem had first set eyes on Chenelle the first day of sixth grade at Banneker Elementary. Her hair was corn-rowed in braids that fell just below her shoulder complemented by a beautifully ornate pattern of beads. Her face so smooth, without blemish, pretty and black, legs long and supple; body displaying hints of the young lady who was now Homecoming Queen. They would talk about how he was afraid to speak to her because of her three older brothers, how he didn't know what to say to impress somebody as cute as she was. One incident he particularly remembered was the story of how her oldest brother, Levar, yanked a boy out of an apple tree because the little fella didn't believe it was "her" tree. "Yeah, you could say I had my bodyguards back in those days!," Chenelle laughed. Sharing the table with Kadeem and Chenelle were Andrea (Cookie) Tisdale and Malik Hammond, Jacques Styles and LaTonya Walker; and filling out the group was Veronica Sapp, who sat next to an empty chair waiting for the arrival of her date, Malcolm Tate, the hero of the evening who scored three touchdowns.

The girls first met in the second grade and were best friends to this day. As eight graders they were runners-up in the local McDonald's Double-Dutch competition. With the newness of High School and the diversity of extra-curricular activities they'd end up pursuing different venues such as majorettes ('Drea), cheerleading (Chenelle), track and field ('Roni) and basketball (LaTonya). This year, their last year, they would combine their talents once again to become the nucleus of the girls track team. Just like the old days. Looking across the ballroom, LaTonya was the first to spot Malcolm coming toward their table. "Roni…," LaTonya teased, "…you know you gotta reward Malcolm for being a hero tonight. Jacques is going to be a happy roughneck tonight and he didn't even play!" Looking over at Jacques she mouthed "not really." "I ain't the girl, girlfriend…," Roni countered. "I don't need the pressure of no baby while I'm going to college and trying out for the Olympic team." "Olympics…?," Cookie laughed. "…and what you gonna do when you get there?" "Set a world record!," Roni answered emphatically raising her right hand as though she was testifying. "You go girl!…," Chenelle put in, "…chaste until I say 'I do'. 'Tonya, you know your daddy would kill you for talking about a roughneck." Malik, Kadeem and Jacques looked at each other, threw up their hands feigning disappointment and laughed. Each of the young men knew the young ladies were right. Although statistics on black teenage pregnancies were exaggerated compared to other races, there were still too many. Each had made a conscious decision to wait until they were men to be a man. Malcolm tiptoed to the table behind Veronica, kissing her on the right cheek.

"Give the brother some love," Malcolm said, as he walked around the table kissing the ladies and hugging the fellas. When he got to Chenelle he knelt and kissed her gloved hand in mock chivalry. "Get up knucklehead!...," Kadeem growled, feigning jealously, "...you just remember who's escorting this queen tonight 'G'!" With the exception of the customary first dance being danced by the homecoming queen, Chenelle and company were waiting for Malcolm's arrival so the whole table would be present on the dance floor. "I Want To Be Down" began to play, enticing all four couples to make way for the dance floor. The four girls began to serenade the young men responsible for making them feel like queens this evening. The group held center stage, dancing beneath the rotating ball hanging from the ceiling. "No matter what time of day..." the music faded to its end. "Cookie, come with me to the bathroom!, Roni said. "Let's all go", 'Tonya added, grabbing Chenelle by the hand and pulling her toward the door leading from the ballroom. "It's a woman thing..." Malik laughed. "...I'm going for some punch, anybody else want some?" "I'm with that Money," Kadeem chimed in. The two made two trips each to the buffet table before the young ladies returned. Malcolm was explaining why her preferred Barry Sanders over Emmitt Smith, when..."I don't give a F@*! if Kadeem is your date. You shoulda came with a real man like me!" "I ain't tryin' to hear this Damon. Why do you have to act a fool all the time?, Chenelle asked in a civil tone. "I don't see why Shayla thinks you're all that anyway. You're always dissin' her in public!, " Cookie added angrily. Before Kadeem, Malik, Jacques and Malcolm got across the dance floor, Coach Hawk was escorting Damon out the door and into the parking lot. "You shouldna' went there Chenelle!," Damon yelled. Shayla discreetly walked into the lobby through a side door and called her daddy with the "mad money" he'd given her in case something like this happened.

IT ALL STARTED WHEN...

It was a beautiful spring day – Cherry Blossoms in bloom outside. The annex of Mason Street A.M.E. Church stood ready for the wedding procession to begin. Damon Edwards stood at the alter beaming brightly, proud of his missing front tooth. His Best Man, Randy (Skipper) Greene, stood just as proud. The four remaining groomsmen, Timmy Jeter, Bobby Jones, Eric Prater and Curtis Mack, took turns thumping each other's ears and jabbing each other with their elbows until Mother Graham whispered from the front row seat, "Little Boys, I'm gonna beat the black offa y'all if ya don't straighten up!" "Yes mam," the boys cowered. Timmy Jeter looked down at his shoes momentarily and then back at Mother Graham who was now shaking her finger at him. He was her favorite of 15 grandchildren.

All the little girls wore carnation pink satin dresses. Their headdresses were adorned with carnations and strings of tiny faux pearls falling over their ears. They were all giggles when

LaTonya showed them how they could see their reflections on their patent leather shoes. Cookie, who was the Maid of Honor, stood waving at Deacon Samuel Tisdale, her daddy. Except for Chenelle, he was her second bestest, favorite person in the world. Next to Cookie stood: LaTonya, then Veronica, with Nadia Grant, Gina (Pooh) Hall, and Phylicia Barnett filling out the sextet. Six beautiful babies - Darlings of the church. "I wish they would hurry up," Damon whispered, just as the first note of "Here Comes the Bride" was struck on the organ. Taking their places on the front row, the Henderson's watched, along with the Edwards and the Mason Street family, as 12 year old Raymond escorted his little sister to the altar and gave her away.

Later at the picnic, Nona would lament on how she'd spent the hour before the wedding repairing the damage the mischievous Jarad had caused to Chenelle's dress; "All those hours shopping for the right notions to make my baby look like a princess bride. That rascal somehow loosened the eye hooks fastening the neck and cut a few extra holes in the train. Micah was some kinda hot girl – I spent just as much time pleading with Micah not to kill him as I did fixing the dress!"

Damon and Chenelle were married in a Tom Thumb wedding on that spring Saturday in May of 1984. Now, as he sat in the center of his bedroom talking with "Wild Irish Rose," Damon looked at the picture of him and Chenelle, him already eight years old and she, almost eight, both finishing second grade. She was supposed to be his tonight, Homecoming 1994. She was supposed to be his always. Married. For life. In his mind anyway. "Momma won't miss this," he told himself. He took the picture from the keepsake album and tore it in two. "She shouldna' went there!"

STRANGER THINGS
HAVE HAPPENED...

"Sophia, you be a good girl today," Page Hamel directed her pet Afghan hound. "Bianca and I have a long day planned today. After school I've got to decorate for the Halloween party and then make the mad dash back here to feed and walk you before it gets too dark." Even though Chamberlain Crossing was a secured deluxe apartment complex in an "adult" community, Bianca Hamel continually preached to her only child, "You can never be too safe." Bianca met Trevor Hamel at an uptown comedy club during her senior year of college. She and a few of her sorority sisters had traveled to New York during Spring Break instead of following the crowd to Florida. Trevor was a self-made man who'd done well for himself in the dog-eat-dog world of Wall Street. He was so smooth. He didn't look a day older than 25, when in actuality he was thirty-five – thirteen years her senior.

As irony would have it, they were married on April Fool's Day of the following year. Page was born on Christmas Eve. The marriage lasted exactly 13 years with Trevor granting an un-contested divorce. After all, he and Virginia Forbes had been having an affair for the last six years of their union, betrayed by her college roommate and sorority sister. Now, four and one-half years later, Halloween 1994, Page finds herself living in a deluxe apartment building with an aging Afghan hound and a mom who insists on being treated like a big sister. Go figure – she's forty!

Page changed Sophia's water, set the burglar alarm, cut through the club house, and preceded to the parking garage, waving at the gate guard as she exited "The city within the city – Chamberlain Crossing." Turning left onto Clinton she began to sing with Desiree, "Listen as your day unfolds…," playing on 104.1, "the City's best Jazz Station." She had no clue of what this day would be like. Although there was a slight chill in the air, Page drove speedily through town with the top down on her navy and white 325i. She didn't notice the speedometer read 50 mph as she rounded the corner onto Marshall Drive, which is a 35 mph zone leading to the student parking lot. Red light. Three blocks from school. First bell in 10 minutes. Not a problem. FLASHING, TWIRLING BLUE LIGHTS WITH INTERMITTENT FLASHES OF RED AND WHITE. "Can I see your license and registration, mam?" "You can't give me a ticket here officer, three blocks from school and first bell…" "Are you speeding right here?…"

Sergeant Simmons interrupted, "...then of course I can and will give you a ticket here where all your little rich friends can see you!" "Thank you very much sir, I hope your day is as peachy as you're making mine!" "Watch yourself Missy, I could do a car search and have my partner frisk you for paraphernalia if you like!" Deciding to cut her losses, Page waited for the officer to finish "doing his job." Accepting her ticket, she drove the remaining distance to school, reporting to Mrs. Fullbright's "Principles of American Government" class exactly eight minutes late—three minutes over the grace period. "I heard about your mishap already, Miss Hamel; Talley began pleading your case as soon as she entered the classroom." "Thanks a lot Miss Newsworthy!," Page sneered at the be speckled Talley Girard. Incidentally, Page and Talley shared the first three classes of each day - their teaming akin to the television friends, Blossom and Six, respectively. Before Page reached her seat in the back of the room, Mason Cole teased, "Must have been those 'Care Free' tags you have that drew the cops' attention." He rubbed Pages' thigh as she passed, his ring leaving a snag in her stocking. "Spawn is too good a name for you maggot. Keep your hands off me or you'll find yourself in the next police line-up!" "You know you love me..." "I'd rather be wrapped in the bosom of Sappho than to remotely entertain a romantic notion of you, dirtball." Not thinking Mason knew the history of Sappho, Page was not prepared for the rumors that would be birthed

from her attempt to insult the intelligence of a "dumb jock."
Happy Halloween.

During second period, Drama, all was going well until
Talley spilled yellow paint on the manuscript for their joint
one-act play. The final blow to this dreaded day came during
last period, Sociology. While she sat at her desk pouting over
the B minus she'd received for her essay on "The Ethnicity of
Religion," Damon, the pepper half of the tandem, called to
her, "Yo Blossom!" "My name is Page, thank you!" "Anyway,
I need to ask you a question after the bell." "Damon…," Mr.
Dupree interrupted, "I'm sure Page would prefer you directed
your attention to the new assignment on the board as would
I." Damon continued as if Mr. Dupree had never spoken
to him. "I need to know how to get blood out of a sheet. I
mean you being the most intelligent pers…," "Mr. Edwards,
fifth period is over for you today. If you should choose to
challenge my decision, I can have you forcibly removed. It's
you call!" "Watch your back," Damon warned Mr. Dupree as
he walked out the rear door of the classroom. "Try peroxide
or bleach," Page whispered, but Damon was already out of
ear shot. "Demonseed indeed," she whispered again, "I hope
he doesn't blame this incident on me."

The dance started at 9:00 p.m. with the usual crowd of
lames, geeks, etc., arriving on time as they abided by their
parental curfews. Page came dressed as Morticia Addams.
The students who began their Friday nights at the football

game started filtering in about 10:45 p.m. with the news of the Panthers' victory over the Taft Knights, 36-33. Damon had redeemed himself for show-boating during last week's Homecoming game by intercepting a tipped pass and scoring the come-from-behind touchdown. The Panthers now had a record of 7 wins – 1 loss. Intermingled with the usual were-wolves, zombies, skeletons, and various other aliens, Page noticed a couple dressed as Steve Urkel and Laura Winslow in cheer-leading garb. Making her way over to the pair, she extended her hand warmly; "Hi Chenelle, I'm Page Hamel. Congratulations on being crowned homecoming queen last week." "Thank you. I remember you from English last year; where is you girl, Talley, at?" "Please, don't remind me of my shadow tonight. I hope she stays at home…!" No sooner had she lamented over her personal P.I.T.A., Page noticed Talley was dressed as Deanna Troy, talking to none other than Mason Cole, dressed as Commander Ryker. "…Anyway, I think you make a nice couple." "Thanks," Chenelle responded as Page disappeared, weaving her way through the dancing students. "Remember Pooh is having a house party," Chenelle reminded Kadeem. "I know. We're out at 11:30 p.m. and you'll most definitely be home by 1:00 a.m. I ain't tryin' to end up with a broken leg tonight." "That happened twelve years ago and Levar lives upstate New York now." "I'm talkin' about your pops," Kadeem laughed. "What do you think about Mrs. Fullbright's extra credit project, Kadeem?" "I was the one who proposed it!," Kadeem answered matter-o-factly.

"I'm scared of you boy...!," Chenelle answered sarcastically. "...Anyway, I was thinking about asking Page to be my partner. What do you think about her?" "She a little 'out of there' sometimes, but she has a lot of good ideas during student council meetings."

Seizing the opportunity to do something different as student council president, Kadeem suggested to Mrs. Fullbright, faculty advisor and head of the history department, to offer an extra credit project called "Meet Thy Neighbor." During Brotherhood week, February, anyone interested would pair up with a partner not living in their neighborhood, spending alternating weekends at each others home. The pair would then do a report comparing their differences and similarities.

Chenelle mingled with the crowd, receiving congratulatory praises from the many students and faculty. Eleven-thirty. Time to jet. They found Page near the girls' locker room entrance talking with Talley, who stood with her left hand in Mason's back pocket, twirling his class ring which dangled for her necklace with her right. "Page, I hope you don't have a problem with Mason and I going steady. Finder keepers..." "Losers weepers indeed. Spawn was never mine to lose. You're doing me the greatest favor a 'friend' could do, Talley!" Kadeem and Chenelle looked at each other quizzically. "Excuse me Page, could I ask you a question?," Chenelle interrupted. "Do you have Mrs. Fullbright...?" "Yes," Page answered, wondering where the conversation was going. "I was wondering if you'd be my partner for the extra credit project?" "Would I?! Page Hamel, Miss High Society, and Chenelle Henderson, Miss Marshall High, sharing an assignment. I'd be delighted." Page hugged Chenelle, thanking her for considering her a worthy partner. "Kadeem, I'd be careful who I let hug my girlfriend. You never know who might have SAPPHIC intentions," Mason laughed. He leered at Page, "Thought I was just a dumb jock, didn't you? Come on Talley. And to think you thought SHE was the model debutante!" Talley looked over her shoulder to see Page standing with her middle finger raised in the air, tears welling up in her eyes. Not wanting to leave Page standing there, obviously hurt and betrayed, Chenelle offered to sit and talk about what had just happened, but Page declined. "I'll be okay. I was just getting ready to go home anyway."

Midnight. Angry. Hurt. Oblivious to the FLASHING, TWIRLING BLUE LIGHTS WITH INTERMITTENT FLASHES OF RED AND WHITE. It wasn't until the officer finally pulled in front of her that Page noticed she was on the wrong side of the street. She followed as the police car returned to the right side of the street and instructed her to pull over. As he approached the BMW parked behind him, Officer Hyatt shined his flashlight through the windshield. Page shielded her eyes until he appeared beside her door. "Mam, I'm going to have to ask you to get out of the car with your license and registration." I'm not drunk officer and I won't be needing a sobriety test!" "I'll be the judge of that mam; blow into this please," Officer Hyatt directed. "Halloween isn't until Monday, mam. Why are you dressed like who is it, Elvira or that Addams Family lady?" Page handed the breathalyzer back to Officer Hyatt and attempted to explain. Finally, noticing he was holding an additional identification card, Officer Hyatt was both agitated and embarrassed to find the "woman" was a high school senior obviously returning from a school dance. "Miss Hamel, you've blown negative, so I'm puzzled as to why you were driving on the wrong side of the road." Now he noticed the tears and the red eyes. "It's been a long day Officer. I wasn't paying attention in my haste to get home and cry in private." "Luckily, young lady, there wasn't any opposing traffic. I'm going to let you off with a warning. Good night and be careful." Officer Hyatt remained parked until Page was a block away, ran her "Carefree" tags, and then decided to follow her after his screen informed him of her ticket just this morning. When she turned into Chamberlain Crossing he shook his head. "Poor little rich girl!," he said. Although she didn't get a second ticket, Page sighed to herself as she undressed and got into the shower, "Lightning does strike twice."

Pooh only lived three blocks from the school – walking distance. "If I could be sure my car wouldn't get jacked, we could walk to Gina's," Kadeem suggested half-heartedly. "So just park it over there in the Circle K parking lot," Chenelle advised, still a little concerned over what Spawn had said about Page. "What do you think Mason meant when he said Page might have Sapphic intentions?" "Sappho was a Greek poetess who supposedly had a strong lesbian following," Kadeem explained. "Most of her poetry was written to her daughter, Cleis. I don't know, maybe the clown pressed up on her, she turned him down and he couldn't get with that so he was trying to get back at her through Talley."

The first car they saw as they rounded the corner onto Bethune Place was Damon's. Purple. Black rag-top TRACKER with gold mags. Dropped. Yellow scarf hanging from the rear view mirror tied in a Tupac knot. Laced through the knot was the familiar purple, black and yellow tassel. The photographer let Damon keep it when he took his graduation pictures. "Cause I got it like dat' 'G'," Damon told T.J. before pulling Shayla to him and ordering her to get a beer from the jeep. "Shayla, it ain't gotta be like that…" "Well it ain't your business, is it Chenelle?!" "…you can do better!" "She has what she wants right here," Damon yelled. "Yo Urkel, keep your girl outta my business!" "If you had some business I might try to accommodate you my brother, but…" "You tryin' to play me punk? We can do this right now…" T.J. jumped between the young men to prevent what he thought would definitely be a bad situation for Kadeem. "It don't have to be all that fellas. Pooh promised her moms it wouldn't be any trouble if she had a party tonight, so let's give the sister her props and not mess it up for her, cool?" Pooh came running up the block calling to the group of teens hoping to see a fight. "Hey, my moms said if y'all don't bring it indoors the party will be over before it starts!" Looking over at Damon glaringly, she put her hand up, letting him know she didn't want to hear his excuse for what almost happened. – Let's digress for a minute-

CURIOSITY

Cookie, Chenelle, 'Tonya and Pooh were all sitting in Pooh's front yard with their dolls pretending to have a tea party when the mailman drove up. "Well, hello ladies, how are you today?" "Fine," the girls answered. "This is for you Little Miss Gina," the postman offered reaching down to hand her the letter. When she looked at the return address Gina began crying, dropped her doll and went inside. Cookie was the first to ask, "What's wrong with Pooh Mr. Mailman?" Chenelle and 'Tonya were next, asking, "did she do something wrong?" At first puzzled, and then embarrassed by his callous error, the postman remembered the return address was that of the State Penitentiary. He should have merely placed the letter in the mailbox, thereby saving Pooh the embarrassment of her new friends knowing her secret. "I'm not sure ladies," he answered weakly, "maybe she'll tell you later." "Mr. Postman," Cookie digressed, "why do you have a jungle hat on?" "That's an easy one young lady, it's to keep the sun out of my eyes," – eyes that wanted to cry along with Little Miss

Gina Hall. As he walked back to his truck, looking back at the window where Pooh stood crying, he waved to her while whispering to himself, "I'm sorry little lady." He drove away, hoping she could somehow hear him. "Bye, Mr. Postman," the girls waved as he drove away.

"Girls, Pooh isn't feeling too good right now. She's going to lay down for awhile, okay?" "Okay, Miss Tracie," the girls answered. "Please tell her we hope she gets better," 'Tonya offered. "Let's go over to my house and finish playing 'hairdresser'!" "If 'Roni didn't have the measles we could go get her and go riding our bikes at the school playground," Cookie lamented, not really wanting to go over 'Tonya's house. Ever since Rufus, 'Tonya's German Shepherd teasingly snapped at her, Cookie dreaded even walking near the house. Ironically, Rufus stayed chained in the backyard most of the time. "You're just a big chicken Andrea Tisdale. I don't want you to come over to my house anyway!," 'Tonya pouted, arms folded across her chest. "Well Chenelle's MY best friend, and then VER-ON-I-CA, and then you, so there," Cookie countered, sticking out her tongue. "Come on Chenelle, my momma baked a chocolate cake last night. We can have some for a snack before we go to the playground!" "Well my momma baked some sweet potato pies," 'Tonya retorted in an attempt not to be outdone and establish her ranking on the friendship ladder.

Damon rode up on his bicycle – almost as if he knew Chenelle needed a way out of this predicament. "Come and see the club house T.J. and I built in the woods!" "Okay, let me get my bicycle." Chenelle immediately ran across the street pass the three houses that separated the Hendersons from the Sapps. Having four brothers, three of them older, Chenelle couldn't help being a tomboy. As Chenelle and Damon rode down Linda Drive towards the woods, 'Tonya and Cookie stood scowling at each other for a few seconds before turning away and walking toward their houses.

"I think that bird over there is a woodpecker," Damon said, pointing at a tree five yards away to their left. Damon led Chenelle twenty yards into the woods, turning 45° to the left and walking another fifty yards before turning 90° to the right where an old ten-speed bicycle frame lay rusting; walking another fifteen yards finally turning 45° to the left and crawling through three feet of bushes hiding the path which lead to the secret fort, ten yards ahead. Chenelle stood in awe, admiring the five-foot-tall wooden structure that stood between two trees standing about ten feet apart. She walked ahead of Damon around the right of the fortress, entering the blue door warning "DO NO ENTER." When Damon heard her scream, he knew she'd seen the fish tank with T.J.'s garter snake in it. "What's wrong Scaredy Cat, ain't you ever seen a snake before?," Damon laughed. "I ain't scared, I just didn't think you had anything in here!," Chenelle proclaimed boldly. "Prove it!," Damon dared taking the snake out of the tank and offering it to her. "Snakes are nasty and I don't have to touch it just to prove to you I ain't scared Damon!" "I knew you wouldn't touch it. My Gam'ma always says boys are made of 'Snakes, Snails and Puppy Dog Tails and girls are made of Sugar, Spice and Everything nice'," Damon continued to taunt. "And you're stupid too, Damon," Chenelle countered, placing her hands on her hips and poking her bottom lip out. "Did you and T.J. build this by yourself?" "Yeah!!!," Damon answered emphatically, when, in reality, it was already there when they wandered upon it just before school ended a month ago. "We found the chair over there by the creek and the rest of this stuff we took from his uncle's junk yard." "Where do you go to the bathroom 'cause I gotta tinkle?!" "We go over by the creek behind the big tree. Come on, I'll show you since you're scared of snakes!" "I told you I ain't scared Damon and if you keep saying that then I'm gonna leave!" "You don't know how to get back to Linda Drive so you can't leave!" Knowing Damon was right Chenelle followed Damon to the "big" tree so she could relieve herself. Chenelle unsnapped her red overalls before she realized Damon was standing next to her. "Go over there and stop trying to watch me, Nasty!" When Damon walked over to a tree about three feet away she squatted down and tinkled. Reaching over and grabbing one of the shiny leaves growing by the tree she dabbed herself dry and stood to fasten her suspenders. When she looked over at Damon who stood partially obscured by the tree, she noticed he was shaking himself. As he turned toward her and begin zipping his pants she asked him, "What were you doing Damon?" "I had to go pee too!" "So why were you standing up?" "Why where you squatting down?" "You wasn't supposed to be watching me, Nasty!" "You was watching me Chenelle!" "I was not. I only saw you when I stood up to snap my pants. Now why were you standing up to go tinkle?," Chenelle demanded. "Because that's how boys go pee!"

Damon had never been to the bathroom with his mother or grandmother so he wasn't aware of the anatomical and mechanical differences between boys and girls. He just knew that girls were not like boys. But Chenelle, on the other hand, lived in a house with four brothers and a father. She had even seen her mother changing Kenyan when all of a sudden his 'willy' squirted water. Nona had explained to her "baby girl" that boys had willies and girls didn't and she wasn't supposed to touch them. "Can I see your willy Damon?" "Only if I get to see yours too!" "Okay, but not out here, somebody else might see us." The two children raced back to the club house excitedly, anxious to see each others "private parts." Damon closed the door behind them and pushed a chair in front of the door just in case T.J. happened by. "You go first Chenelle since my Gam'ma says ladies before gentlemen!" "Uh, ah, you might try to trick me Damon. We have to do it at the same time." "Okay...," Damon agreed, "...when I count to three we will pull down our pants." Damon counted to three slowly giving them both time to gather their courage, after all, this was different from going to the bathroom. This was a NO NO!!!

One.   Two.   Two an' a half.

Fruit of the Loom meet Pastel Butterflies. At first Damon was disappointed because Chenelle's "willy" was obviously not there. Then Chenelle spread her feet apart and pointed between her legs. "Wow" was all Damon said.

It was 1:00 pm. T.J. had waited long enough for Damon to come by so they could go catch some bugs and things to feed the snake. Mother Graham didn't mind him having a snake, he just couldn't have that "devils pet" in her house. He spent the summer with her because he was her favorite grand baby. He collected a whole mayonnaise jar of lady bugs, pincher bugs, potato bugs (rollie-poleys), and stink bugs by himself. Off to the woods he rode at light speed to empty the jars' contents into the tank with the snake. At first he tried to push the door open but it wouldn't budge. Hearing some voices through the door he decided to pull a crate under the only window the club house had. "Sometimes at night I tickle myself before I go to sleep. It feels funny," Chenelle confided. "My mom always tells me… 'Stop playing with that thing boy' when she sees me holding myself. Then she tells me to go use the bathroom," Damon shared exchanging confidences. T.J. stood on the wobbly crate and looked over the lip of the window seal just as the two children took each others offer to touch one another. Jealous, T.J. jumped down off the crate, ran around to the door and pushed with all his might, flinging it open. Caught, literally, "with their pants down," Chenelle and Damon scrambled to fix their clothes and begged T.J. not to tell. "I won't tell if I get to do everything Damon got to do!" "No T.J., I don't like you!" "I'm gonna count to ten and then I'm gonna run and tell your momma I saw you and Damon playing house. One, Two…" When he got to five, Timmy noticed the lid on the fish tank was open. He stopped counting and walked over to the tank. Seizing the moment, Chenelle darted from the club house and down the trail toward the bush hiding the secret entrance. "You let the snake get away Damon," T.J. yelled angrily. He pushed Damon, causing him to fall over the bean bag chair sitting in the middle of the floor. The two boys rolled around on the floor throwing an occasional punch. In the back of both of their minds they felt tough like the guys on television. One of Damon's punches connected with T.J.s left eye. Hurt, snake gone, T.J. ran out of the club house, out of the woods down Linda Drive, right onto Evers Street and into the third garage on the right. Mother Graham was in the kitchen starting the food for tomorrow's church dinner when Timmy came through the door with his hand cupped over his eye. "What happened to you baby?," she asked. Not wanting to be a tattle-tale, T.J. answered in the usual manner. "Nothing." Honor among thieves. Not wanting to force the issue, Mother Graham left it alone, nursed Timmy's eye and continued preparing the meal for tomorrow. Experience assured the truth would come out later. When Timmy didn't respond to her question, "where's Damon?," she knew they'd probably had a disagreement.

All went well the rest of the afternoon and evening, on through breakfast Sunday morning. All excepting Timmy awoke with a black eye. Chenelle woke up crying with a terrible rash over her privates and was allowed to miss Sunday School and Church. Timmy was forced to tell his grandmother what happened at the club house. The Edwards were TOLD about their little devil and Nona received a phone call after church advising her to talk to her "fast little girl." "Thank you, Mother Graham…," Nona responded graciously. "…I think having poison ivy is punishment enough." Having gone through this numerous times before with her sons, Nona had seen Poison Ivy enough to write a book about it. Chenelle wound up missing a week of school, the club house was torn down and only Damon knows who gave HIM his black eye. Curiosity indeed. – back to the party.

Before their shouting match began to take shape of a definite fight, Damon had said a few thought-provoking things to Kadeem. One statement, in particular, upset him terribly. Kadeem wanted to ask what Damon meant when he said "…if you were taking care of your girl like I was…," but he decided to leave well enough alone. He had to make sure Chenelle met her 1:00 AM curfew. He would find out the truth soon enough. Chenelle said little as they walked back to Circle K and even less on the way to her house. Kadeem was somewhat surprised when he pulled into the driveway triggering the automatic lighting running the length of the drive and walk ways to the front porch.

Mr. Henderson had the system installed earlier in the week to serve a two-fold purpose; lighting system, and to discourage potential intruders during late hours of the night. "Good night Kadeem," Chenelle said before kissing him on the cheek and getting out of the car. Puzzled, Kadeem got out of the car also but stood and watched as Chenelle unlocked the front door, turned to wave, then disappeared into the safety of home. As Kadeem backed out of the driveway he whispered as if Chenelle was still sitting beside him, "I'll call you tomorrow, okay?"

Although Chenelle didn't acknowledge her father's presence, she knew he always sat in the den until all his children were safe at home. On her pillow she found a box of chocolates with a card tucked beneath the lavender bow adorning it. It was from Daddy. Inside was a little note which said: "My dear Baby Girl, you are almost a woman now and soon to be leaving us for college and the temptations of being 'grown.' It is hard for a father to watch his daughter grow into a woman, especially his only one, but I'm learning. Sleep well and I'll see you in the morning. P.S., I really like Kadeem." Hearing footsteps go pass her bedroom door, she whispered, "Good night Daddy," not expecting him to respond. Micah continued down the hall to his bedroom and crawled into bed. Nona rolled over and kissed him saying, "Thank you for being such a good man." Before Chenelle dozed off to sleep she read the card once again and spoke to the card, proxy for her daddy, "I like him too!" Then she cursed herself for ever liking Damon. Ten years ago. Puppy love.

"What's up?," Kenyan spoke into the phone. "Yo Kenny, its Kadeem, is Chenelle awake yet?" "Hold on, I'll check." The phone slipped from his hand as he attempted to place it on the counter. Kenyan cringed, imagining the bang Kadeem heard on the other end. "Chenelle, Kadeem is on the phone," he screamed down the hall. "Tell the brother I dropped the phone by accident, okay?," he added as a postscript.

It was 10:00 AM. Saturday, the 29th of October. Everybody was coming home to surprise Nona for her 50th birthday. "Hi," Chenelle spoke in to the phone. "I'm sorry for how everything turned out last night, Damon can be such an…" "I don't want to talk about Damon right now Chenelle. You don't need to apologize for how he acted. I just feel sorry for Shayla," Kadeem interrupted before asking Chenelle what her plans were for the day. "We're having a surprise party for my mom this afternoon when all my brothers get home. Why don't you come over so you can meet Levar and Raymond?" "Okay," Kadeem accepted, "But until then why don't we go to Mason Park and talk or check out a movie at West Lake. You can bring your crew too!," he added, remembering that

Chenelle and Cookie were close to inseparable. 'Roni and 'Tonya were still close but not as close as Cookie was. Bestest friends for life. "Okay, I'll call Cookie and tell her to meet us in the food court and then we'll decide which movie we want to see. Pick me up at 12:00PM, okay?" "I'll be there at 11:45AM!" After Chenelle hung up, she fixed herself a bowl of Captain Crunch with Crunch Berries and sat down at the counter separating the kitchen from the family room. "Good morning Baby Girl, I trust you had a good time last night?," Micah smiled at his daughter inquisitively. "It was alright until Damon tried to get Kadeem to fight him. I probably caused the argument when I told Shayla she could do better than Damon." "I'm so glad you got over your 'puppy love' with that thug before you started high school Baby. I don't know if I could've handled him visiting these last four years." "Where have you been Daddy?," Chenelle admonished, "Damon and I haven't liked each other since the sixth grade!" If he only knew what prompted her disdain for her childhood sweetheart he'd probably be in prison right now. "Anyway, Chenelle, I'm glad you and Kadeem seem to be doing so well. Is he coming over today for the…" "Shhh Daddy, Momma has ears that can hear an ant whisper. Yes, Kadeem's coming over in about an hour and we're going to go to the matinee with Cookie, Roni and 'Tonya if that's okay with you, of course?," Chenelle half told/asked her Daddy before winking at him teasingly. "You're a mess Little Girl," Micah laughed.

Swatting the air in Chenelle's direction while walking toward the den, he finished, "I gotta pay some bills!"

Kadeem pulled into the driveway at precisely 11:45AM. Chenelle met him at the door yelling back to her parents, "I'm gone!" "Did you call Cookie and the gang?," Kadeem asked, while admiring Chenelle dressed in a pair of Dickies overalls, a Vikings sweat shirt and the off-white/purple billed Marshall High baseball cap. Of course the front of the ball cap had the fighting panther encrusted on it. Tomboy but definitely girl. "I didn't let you get to the door because my father would still be telling you how much he likes you when my brothers got here this afternoon. Cookie and 'Tonya don't want to go to the movies so 'Roni and I gave in to going to Mason Park and listening to D.J. Freeze kick-off his 'Halloween in the Park Party Mix.'" "I forgot about that. The park is gonna be full of fools but it'll probably be on!" While they drove toward the park they also listened to 101.9, WMIX "Radio from the 'Hood." "D.J. Freeze here in the park 'til after dark, givin' it to ya good, alllll the way from the hood, come out and give somebody a shout out." Kadeem looked at Chenelle and the two began to laugh. "That brother is stoopid," Chenelle started, but was interrupted by a voice from the radio. "Yo, this is Demon Seed, the meanest, nastiest outside linebacker in the city and I'm givin' a shout out to the Marshall High Panthers. Me and my boy, Spawn, put in some work every Friday and we want everybody else to know we in the house, peace!" "And that boy is a fool!," Kadeem added. Hearing

Damon's tirade reminded him of the question burning inside begging to be answered. Now was as a good a time as any he thought. "Chenelle, what did Damon mean when he said he was taking care of you last night?" "I don't want to go there now, Kadeem. Damon ruined last night, don't let him get in your head today, please?!" "Is it that bad that you can't tell me about it?," Kadeem continued. "Look Kadeem, we have only been dating since school started. Damon and I go back to second grade there's a lot of stuff I don't want to remember much less talk about right now, okay? I like you but you don't need to know my life story after being my boyfriend for only three months. Let's just have a nice time at the park with the gang okay?" She reached over and placed her hand over Kadeem's right hand, angrily squeezing the steering wheel of his 90' Jetta GLI. "Cool," Kadeem agreed trying to rid himself of the anger he felt at his timing in asking Chenelle such a question because of a stupid statement made by an "immature boy" during a stupid agreement. Jealously. Curiosity. Anger. Not a nice beginning to a potentially beautiful day.

JUDAS
(Anger)

Mason Park wasn't as crowded as they thought it would be. Both Chenelle and Kadeem knew that wouldn't be the story around 2:00 PM. The air was still a little tense between them. Each wrestled with the silence holding them captive for the remainder of the drive to the park. Chenelle broke the silence saying, "Tonya said to meet over by the Tennis courts at 12:30 PM." As if on cue, Kadeem reached out and took Chenelle's left hand in his right, wrapping their arms around her waist. Chenelle reciprocated by interlacing her fingers with his and gently squeezing their knuckles together. Though this latest exchange was non-verbal the message was clear. The peace had been struck. Silence is Golden, but sometimes silence is dangerous.

Down the path to the tennis courts, Kadeem and Chenelle walked, oblivious to the two couples watching them from the parking lot near the swimming pool. Damon and

Shayla. Mason and Talley. At Damon's feet lay an eighty pound Rottweiler; his Christmas present from his Gam'ma two years ago. She'd bought it for him when the family moved into Killian Forest. This was his father's present to the family after he became a partner in one of the city's most prominent orthodontics practices. Homes in the upper 400's. There had been death threats. "I don't have time to find out if it's just a bunch of teenagers playing a joke or, if it's some disgruntled redneck unhappy with US moving into THEIR neighborhood," his Gam'ma had said. "Oh, if Vincent were still alive he'd be so proud of you Linford!" Damon remembered his Gam'ma saying to his father, her eldest son, as he carried his wife Sharon across the threshold to their new home. Then he carried Gam'ma. A Raisin in the Sun. Linford Edwards had made good on his promise to do better by his family than his father had. Now two years hence, his son Damon lay in wait to do an injustice to another young man because an unrequited "puppy love" had grown into an obsession. "Hey Mason, help me have some fun." "Sure, I'm game for anything," the pony-tailed miscreant laughed. "Ow," Damon screamed feeling the sting from Shayla pinching his arm. "Why don't you just let it go Damon. You act like Chenelle is the only girl in the world. She ain't all that, anyway. I don't care if she is Homecoming Queen…" "You can walk anytime you get ready. You ain't all that either. You should be glad I'm lettin' you hang with me, hello?!" The sting of Damon's retort brought Chenelle's voice back to her, "…Shayla you could do better!" Mason and Talley stood silent during this brief exchange. "Come on Spawn, let's see where the love birds are going." Yanking the dog's leash, Damon nodded at Mason and proceeded to follow Kadeem and Chenelle down the trail. "Wait a minute, I need to go back to my jeep to get something before we go," Damon yelled to Spawn. He reached into the cooler in the back of the jeep and pulled out a six pack of Coke. "What's that for Demonseed?," Mason asked as he started to feast on the excitement of the moment. "You'll find out in a minute," Damon laughed.

As they rounded the corner leading to the tennis courts Kadeem noticed Malik, Malcolm, and Jacques tossing a football. The girls where spreading a cloth over one of the picnic tables. "Ooops, I forgot to tell you to stop by the bakery and get some donuts, Kadeem." "Well, I hope they forgive us for not bringing anything. We can go and get some if they really want us to. Let's go let them know we're here, okay?" "I forgot to tell Kadeem to stop by the bakery because we got into an argument about Damon," Chenelle began to apologize but was interrupted when Malcolm said, "Speak of the Devil and he appears." Damon and Mason were walking up the trail slowly pointing at the group standing around the table laughing. "What do you want Cole?," Malcolm asked angrily. "Me and Demonseed just wanna have some fun. Is it okay with you Mr. Barry Sanders wannabe?" "Mr. Tate to you punk!" "Fellas, fellas, we're teammates," Damon teased sarcastically. "It's all good. I brought these sodas as a peace offering between me and Kadeem." And then it happened just as he and Spawn had rehearsed. "To prove how sincere I am about this, I'm going to show you with a kiss." Damon hugged Kadeem then walked away, turned and threw one of the sodas toward him. When Kadeem reached to catch the soda Mason unhooked the leash from around the dog's neck and stood back as the 80lb dog leaped into the air and grabbed Kadeem around the wrist while attempting to catch the soda can. Kadeem's scream wasn't as nauseating as the sound of his bones cracking under the pressure of the dogs' jaws. "Let him go, Judas," Damon shouted. Kadeem let go of the soda can. "My bad man, I forgot he likes to play catch with soda cans," Damon laughed. He and his minion walked away as the group huddled around Kadeem.

"I didn't think you were that crazy Damon. You're going to have a hard time explaining this to the police." "Not so good brother. All you have to do is be my amen corner!" Mason was definitely shaken by what had just transpired but he couldn't let his cohort in crime know. "Damon," Jacques hollered, "I'm going to kick your @*# after we get Kadeem to the doctor. No, no," Jacques continued, "I'm going to kick your @*# now!" Malik grabbed him before he could run after Damon and Mason. Malcolm had immediately run to call 911 when he realized was happening. After placing the 911 call, he also ran to find the police. Damon and Mason were just a little bit surprised when the police met them at the entrance to the park along with the ASPCA. "Surrender the dog peaceably Mr. Edwards or we'll put him to sleep right here on the spot," the mounted officer warned. "Do you young ladies have a ride home; your boyfriends are going downtown!" Once again Shayla would end up calling her father because of Damon. Looking over at the ambulance she could see Chenelle walking beside the gurney on which Kadeem lay. The look she got from Chenelle brought back thoughts of last night, "Shayla, you could do better!" The Betancourts were called and advised to meet Kadeem at Community Hospital; the Edwards and Coles to meet their delinquents at the Park Precinct.

The air was very strained when the parents, Cole and Edwards, signed the forms to have their sons released pending arraignment. "I have a good mind to leave you here, Damon, after pulling an asinine stunt like this boy!," Linford chided. Sharon interjected, "This isn't the time or place to discuss your disgust with our son, Edwards!," she herself just as hurt by her baby's latest shenanigan. "Rest assured Linford," Grant Cole offered, "these two won't be palling around with each other for a while. With any luck the Betancourts won't press charges!" Demonseed and Spawn, still refusing to see the gravity of the situation, attempted to 'low five' each other as they were leaving the station. They reconsidered that endeavor when Grant Cole, who bore a spooky resemblance to Howie Long, stepped between them, grabbed Mason by the elbow, and politely ushered his spawn toward the door. "I'll call you this evening, Linford, after I talk with Betancourt." "I will offer to pay the medical expenses when I speak with him later," Linford informed Grant, "but yea, we'll talk later!" Linford nodded to his wife and the Edwards followed the Coles out of the precinct. Not a word was spoken during the drive to either home. Each family decided to wait until they'd spoken to Walter Betancourt before pursuing this matter further.

Kadeem was diagnosed with a fracture of the distal head of his right radius complicated by a dislocation of the Scaphoid, Trapezium, and Trapezoid bones of the wrist. He would leave the hospital wearing a short arm acrylic cast, arm sore from the tetanus shot he received and a little perturbed with Chenelle for ever giving Damon a reason to think he owned her! "I'll see you at school Monday Chenelle. I don't think I'd be much of a guest at your mother's party this afternoon. The brother turned his dog on me because I'm talking to you Chenelle!" "Calm down son," Ramona Betancourt interrupted. "It's not her fault! Come on Chenelle, let me get you home. I'm sorry K.D. is upset with you but in light of the circumstances you have to understand." Chenelle reached out to hug Kadeem. After his tirade, she was afraid he would refuse her affection. When he responded in kind, she smiled at Mrs. Betancourt. "Let me go call my parents." "I'll meet you in the lobby Baby." "Daddy, I'm at the hospital with Kadeem…" "I know Babygirl, Kenny told us what happened. Should I come get you or should I send one of your brothers?" "No Daddy, I'm going to ride with Mrs. Betancourt. Jacques drove Kadeem's car here. Don't worry, I won't be late for the party." "We'll see you when you get her Love," "Okay Daddy."

Once again Damon had spoiled Chenelle's day. If it weren't for the fact that her family would be celebrating her mother's fiftieth birthday it would be totally ruined. After Mrs. Betancourt dropped her off, Chenelle remembered she still needed to buy her mother a birthday present. Wanting to catch up on the latest gossip about who was dating whom and how many knuckleheads were trying to hit on his sister and ex-girlfriend Amina, Jarad offered to drive Chenelle to the mall. "So, Nelle, what's up with you and Kadeem? Is that fool Damon still tryin' to get with you?" When Chenelle didn't answer right away Jarad knew his sister was upset. "Jay," Chenelle began, voice shaking, "Damon is sick! I don't know what to do to make this fool get the point that I could care less if he lived or died!" "Be careful Babygirl, you might get what you wish and then you'd never forgive yourself for thinking that way!," Jarad cautioned. Chenelle reached into the glove compartment for the numbered hand towel Jarad had worn as a Panther receiver and wiped her eyes. "I'm just so tired of Damon and his B.S." Jarad poked Chenelle in the ribs and told her not to worry; he'd make it all good.

Chenelle and Jarad ran into Chelsea McDavid at the mall. Jarad had been the object of her desire since the beginning of her freshmen year when she and Chenelle were the only freshmen Junior Varsity cheerleaders. She'd befriended

Chenelle as a means of being close to Jarad who was the Junior Varsity quarterback. Chenelle declined Chelsea's invitation to her Halloween party. Jarad promised he'd make an appearance, if it was okay with his mom, since her birthday was the reason he'd come home. "A lot of the football team is going to be there," Chelsea offered as a means of assuring Jarad he'd made the right choice.

Chelsea's father owned and operated four photography studios and had a contract with the school to shoot graduation, prom and sporting event pictures. One of Chelsea's favorite pictures was one of her running onto the field and leaping into Jarad's arms after he'd thrown a come-from-behind touchdown with fifteen seconds on the clock. It adorned her vanity even today three years hence, she with her legs wrapped around him as he stood with his helmet raised into the air. Now she was the cheerleading captain, the logical choice for captain after Chenelle had announced she wouldn't be cheerleading during their senior year. Their friendship was a bittersweet one at best. For three years she'd tried to get Jarad to see her as more than just a cheerleader but to no avail. It hurt so much when he told her how cute she was but "I'm just not the brother to have jungle fever." She thought he'd changed his mind when he decided to come to her party but he'd had a secret agenda all along.

Why does everything have to revolve around Chenelle Henderson," she asked the mirror before going to bed.

Chenelle would hear how Jarad ruined her party. Never had anyone embarrassed her so much. First he disses her by telling her she is "cute" but he doesn't date white girls, and then he comes to her house just to punch somebody out.

Monday. First Bell. Talley was confiding to Page she'd made a mistake getting involved with Mason when the two terrors came to the classroom entrance. "You can't punk out on me now Cole, I thought we was boys thick and thin?!" "Look man, my dad took the keys to my truck. Now I have to ride the school bus until Christmas. Two months riding the bus with a bunch of deadbeat, lames. I ain't weak man but I want my truck back!" "I knew you weren't as down as you pretended to be. Ole sorry #@! white boy!" "Who's sporting a black eye ole bad #@! black boy?!," Mason laughed. "You better push on before you're late for art class Picasso!" "You didn't do it punk so you better watch your mouth before you find yourself with one just like this fool!," Damon warned while trying to save face with the other students standing in the hall. Cookie had just rounded the corner in route to the bathroom when she witnessed the exchange between the two thugs. She couldn't wait to find Chenelle and tell her what she'd seen. "You should see his eye. BLACK. BLACK. BLACK.!" Chenelle laughed to herself remembering Jarad had told her he'd make it all good.

Save for the verbal exchange between Damon and Mason Cole, the school day was progressing as usual. However, as the noon hour approached the cafeteria was abuzz with a potential confrontation between Chenelle and Chelsea. "Hey Ken, I heard Chelsea McDavid is going to get in your sisters @#* during lunch," offered an anonymous blue eyed freshman. "I don't know who you are Bud, but if you're one of her friends you better tell her she would rather slap a grizzly bear than to step to 'Nelle!" Concerned, but not worried, Kenyan sought his sister out to inform her of her impending showdown. "What's up Baby Brother?," Chenelle teased as Kenyan approached her locker. "Oh some little blue-eyed fool just told me Chelsea McDavid was planning to step to you during lunch. I'm not worried about you but I thought you might want to know." "Good lookin' out Kenny. I don't know what her problem is but she better recognize!" "Seee ya sister, watch your back!" "I ain't worried about her," Chenelle assured her brother. "I feel ya 'Nelle," he shouted running to Spanish class.

Much to the disappointment of the few students who were expecting to see a fight at noon, Chelsea reconsidered confronting Chenelle. She had ample time to play out the drama in her mind with vivid images of LaTonya, Andrea, and Veronica standing beside Chenelle, cautioning her to re-think her plans. Later in the day however, Chelsea would find an ally where she least expected – Gina Hall. Although Gina didn't particularly like Chelsea, she also was angry at Chenelle for being the center of attention at her party. For eleven years she had watched Damon's obsession with Chenelle grow in addition to being the odd one out, the fifth friend of the foursome.

Because of her budding interest in photography, Pooh joined the staff of the school paper and yearbook during her junior year. From time to time Mr. McDavid would invite promising students to help with the developing and selection of the snapshots to be submitted to the local paper and booster clubs that supported the school's extra-curricular activities. Gina's work was selected numerous times to be exhibited alongside Mr. McDavid's. Unfortunately, even with the notoriety she received for her pictures, Gina wasn't as popular as she wanted to be. Somebody had to put Chenelle in check. She could help Chelsea get her revenge and no one would be the wiser.

"Chelsea, can I talk to you?," Gina called as she approached her in the student parking lot. Chelsea recognized Gina immediately and waved her over. She was curious as to why, after hardly ever talking to her during the time she spent at her father's shop, Gina suddenly wanted to talk. "What do you want to talk to me about, Pooh?" "My name is Gina girlfriend! Only the people from my neighborhood call me Pooh!" "I'm sorry," Chelsea answered defensively, "I thought that's what you liked to be called!" "Anyway, I heard you want to get back at Chenelle for what Jarad did at your party…" "And?," Chelsea answered coyly. "Well I have a plan…" "I was going to McDonald's, we can talk there if you want. My treat!" "Let's go!," Gina agreed.

Chelsea deliberated over her filet of fish and orange juice eagerly listening to Gina's plan. "If I can get her to come to my slumber party in two weeks we can make sure her Thanksgiving is anything but nice." "So what do I do, Gina?" "You just have to be patient, Chelsea. I've been planning my revenge for a while." "Okay, I can wait. You just make sure you get her there." The two young ladies smiled at each other, content with the possibility of exacting a joint revenge on 'Miss All That.' Suddenly, remembering she was supposed to meet Miss Lamay to discuss the cheers and uniforms for the basketball season, Chelsea offered Gina a ride home. Gina declined. "I can catch the #9, it runs right pass my house." Her real reason for declining Chelsea's offer was to eliminate cause for suspicion as to why the two were suddenly hangin' out.

Instead of going directly home, Pooh decided to go by her mother's salon. Sojourners Salon was her favorite place to go and collect her thoughts whenever she wasn't experimenting with new ways to get better shots. She would sit for hours reading EBONY, ESSENCE and JET magazines, drawing inspiration from the advice columns and feature articles dealing with experiences of both popular and everyday black women. The men featured in the Brother to Brother column reassured her that there were many good men to be found, in spite of the prevailing negative media and gossip she heard in her mother's shop.

"Cookie, don't you let anything happen to my car!" "I won't, Momma. Why you always gotta sweat a sista?" "Don't play with me little girl, you could be riding the bus!" Andrea ran over to her mother, gave her a big hug and said, "You wouldn't do your baby like that, would you?" "You just take care of my Maxima 'Miss Thing'! Your daddy would have a cow if he knew I let you drive my birthday present to school but fuss when he wants to use it to drive 'round the corner talkin' about his Town Car is too big!" "Momma I'm gonna be late if you don't give me the keys. 'Tonya and Chenelle are waiting…" "Bye girl," Missionary Tisdale laughed, kissing her daughter on the forehead before guiding her toward the door. Off to school.

Although the final selections for the girls' varsity basketball team were a few weeks away, many potential players were attending the practices after school. 'Tonya was the logical team captain at point and/or shooting guard, depending on who was in the back court with her. Chenelle sat in the bleachers doing her homework, occasionally laughing at her second 'bestest' friend labor up and down the court, running wind sprints. "You oughta be out her with us Miss Thing," 'Tonya called to Chenelle. "Then you could share my pain!" "No thanks, girlfriend, track season will be here soon enough!" Chenelle's focus returned to her homework, at least on the surface. It wasn't until 'Tonya came running into the bleachers after an errant basketball that she realized she was singing, "I wanna be down," with so much emotion that there was no doubt her thoughts were on Kadeem. "You buggin' girl, but it's all good. He'll come around soon," 'Tonya assured her life-long friend. "I'm gonna go take my shower and then we can go, okay?" Chenelle nodded, never lifting her head from her books. Not even one of her inner-circle friends could see her crying on this day.

Miss Olivia Bennett taught freshmen English, was the assistant director of the majorettes, and the assistant for the girls' tennis team. She was a Marshall High alumni, who in spite of her modesty, was the most promising tennis player the city had ever produced. Tennis was both good to her and for her, in that it fostered the confidence and independence she needed to mature into the beautiful Nubian woman she was. Her reddish-brown locked tresses fell neatly over either side of her face, sculpting her pecan complexion to queen-like perfection – smooth and oval. Though she thanked God everyday for loving grandparents, she cursed Him at times for taking her mother before she could know her. Whatever redeeming qualities her father had, her grandparents would never acknowledge; they never forgave him for ruining their baby's life, leaving them to raise her, when they should have been able to enjoy the baby from a distance. The child came before they were ready. So beautiful at times and at other times so ungrateful. Sometimes you could see the resemblance she bore to, "that" @*!# boy! During her sophomore year of high school she occasionally hyphenated her last name making her father's name hers. Those childish spurts of rebelliousness would bring her grandparents to tears. Even now, at twenty-six years old, she had to explain herself to them whenever she opted to place her father's name after the Bennett name on most of her official papers. Why did they agree to tell her who her father was when she reached puberty? They were good to her, in spite of the circumstances that cast her into their lap. God bless them. They were in the early part of their septuagenarian years. Alzheimer's was creeping in. Only God knows how much longer they would live. She granted them a bittersweet victory leaving her name as Bennett. What's in a name, anyway?

Chenelle and 'Tonya practically knocked Miss Bennett down as they exited the locker room, both trying jump through the door before it slammed shut. She and Andrea were discussing the half-time routine for Friday's game while walking to the gym to meet up with the girls. "Ladies, I would expect my English students to behave like this not two people who are hoping to graduate this year!" "No, she didn't go there," 'Tonya whispered, loud enough for Miss Bennett to hear. "Oh yes she did!," Miss Bennett retorted just as sarcastically as 'Tonya had. Chenelle quickly squashed the ensuing cat fight by offering a sophomoric apology. "We're sorry, Miss Bennett. How's the choreography for next week's game coming? I know you and 'Drea are going to have those sistas workin' it!" Knowing she'd been played, however politely, Miss Bennett accepted the flimsy apology and warned the pair to "...just be careful." When the three girls were about ten feet away from the teacher they looked at each other, turned in Miss Bennett's direction, pointed and yelled, "PMS!" Then they ran like they used to when they were in the second grade.

"Ooh girl, your momma is going to die after she kills you!" "SSSshh...ugar, Honey, Iced Tea!" Cookie exclaimed, grabbing Chenelle by the arm. They couldn't believe their eyes. The driver's side window was gone. They ran to the car to see how much more damage was done. When they reached the car and didn't find any glass on the ground, they realized Cookie had forgotten to roll the window up. Their relief was short-lived. A black cat with a litter of thirteen kittens lay curled in the drivers' seat. Chenelle looked at Cookie ashamedly and pronounced, "God don't like ugly."

The somber Monday specter spared no one. Nona was livid when she arrived home. In addition to suffering through rush-hour traffic, standing in a long line to pay for gas, only to lose the ten dollars she owed, she pulled into the driveway to find her precious Sade clawing and barking at the front door. Raymond's girlfriend Phyllicia, had given her the puppy last Christmas as a sort of peace offering. She had called Ray a Momma's boy after he decided to run a errand for his sick momma before coming over to find out what some knucklehead said about her jeans. Anyway, Nona was none too happy to see the puppy on the porch barking and clawing at the door when somebody should be home to let her in. "Kenny," she thought aloud.

"Come here, baby. Momma will let you in." The dank smell wafting from the front room as she entered the foyer confirmed her suspicion. "Kenyan Royce Henderson, if you don't get these smelly size eleven boats out of my front room...!" Kenyan unwittingly put a finger to his mouth, as if to quiet his mother, then informing her he was talking to Tange'. "I don't care who you're talking to. I said get your shoes out of my front room. And what do you mean by let's do a little sumpin', sumpin'?" He wasn't aware of how long Nona had been home or what she had heard, but he knew she didn't really want an answer. He knew needed to act quickly to diffuse the situation at hand. "Look, Tange', I'll hit you back later." Kenyan hurriedly replaced the phone onto the receiver. "Let me give you some love, Ma. I haven't seen you all day," Kenyan joked, reaching out to his mother. "I don't want no ole Judas kiss from you boy. Didn't you hear the baby scratching at the door?" "That mutt was chewing on my Filas so I put her on the porch!" "You should have put them in your room instead of leaving them out here, knucklehead. Don't be mistreating my baby anymore!" As if on cue, Sade turned and barked at Kenyan. "Shut up mutt!," Kenyan warned, stomping his feet at Sade who was now prancing down the hall on Nona's heels. "Boy, you can barely pee straight and talking about a little sumpin' sumpin'." Then she laughed. "Put those shoes outside so they can get some air!" Though Nona was speaking into the air, Kenyan understood the message in her last utterance. She wanted him to know she wasn't happy with his conversation.

Tuesday and Wednesday passed without anything out of the ordinary happening. Thursday however, started a snow ball in motion that wouldn't stop until the beginning of Christmas vacation. Heike Graham had no sooner walked out of the bathroom across from the language lab when she bumped into none other than Mr. Damon Edwards. True to form, Damon proceeded to brag about his sexual prowess and what he could do for her. Heike was able to ignore his immature banter until his cockiness let him make one of the most infantile and cliché statements she'd heard all year. "Hey Red, you know they say the way to find out a woman's true hair color is to look at her Triangle of Venus. Heike just glared at him. "So…," Damon continued, "when you gonna let me peep yours?!" "Step off, Damon!" "What did you say B…?" Before he could shape his lips to finish the "B" word, Heike cut him off. "Don't even go there, my brother. I ain't Queen Latifah, but I'll step to you just as quick if you call me out of my name!" "Set it off B@*#@!"

The knee that was meant for his crotch hit him in the thigh, but the slap against his right ear hit its mark. Mr. Simone detected the first hint of trouble brewing when he noticed the students in the rear of the class staring into the hallway. The tone of the girls' voice alerted him to the urgency of the situation. He reached the hallway and strode between the two teens before the boy could retaliate. "Get to your class young man, before this turns into a situation neither of you need or want! What's this all about anyway?" Damon's first thought was to go through the teacher, but he thought again. Mr. Simone wasn't a small man. The sting went away almost immediately. The ringing in his ear lasted through the day. The dizziness that came with the ringing made his stomach so queasy that he had to excuse himself during fourth bell to save him from further embarrassment by losing his lunch in front of the class.

Football practice wasn't nice for Damon, either. The news of his being rescued by Mr. Simone spread like wildfire. He arrived at practice to find a cheerleader's uniform on his locker with a note pinned over the panther. "Go ahead, Demonseed, read it," Spawn laughed. Damon opened the note and began to read. "If you cant' handle your business like a playa, maybe you ought to be wearing this!" "Who put this up here?" "It was here when we go here, playa," was the collective response he got from his teammates. It only got worse. It seemed like every running play came into his zone without the defensive line slowing down any of the blockers. This left Damon to make every play by himself. The corner backs and defensive ends seemed to be allowing the receivers to come right across the middle, leaving him to easily intercept every pass, only to be gang-tackled by the offense. The coaches kept hollering, "Make the play, Edwards, make the play!" Finally, while he lay on his back with the constant ringing in his ear, he looked into what seemed to be, the eight whirling faces of Coach Hawk and realized it was all planned. Coach Hawk reached out his hand to help him up while scolding, "My All City middle linebacker got his butt kicked by a girl. With all the press about jocks beating their wives and girlfriends, you can ill afford to be labeled as a woman beater before you even graduate from high school. I've got half a mind to bench you tomorrow for making such a fool of yourself. Did you know some scouts are going to be here tomorrow for the game? I won't help you lose a scholarship; you're going to have to do that yourself. Now get off this field and go home. Practice is over for you today!" When Coach let go of Damon's hand, he fell square on his butt. Coach knew then that Damon would not play in Friday night's District Championship game. He had suffered a mild concussion and would not be allowed to suit up for 72 hours. Fortunately, the Panthers won the District game, advancing to the regional play-offs the following week.

Damon played with a vengeance causing five fumbles, one of which he recovered and ran in for a touchdown. With the score being 21-20 the St. Julius Cardinals of Franklin County attempted to kick the winning field goal only to have the tandem of Edwards and Cole jump up and block it. By assuring the team advanced to the Quarter Final

Championships, Damon was again confident there was a scholarship in his future. Hopefully, the letters from the colleges would begin pouring in shortly after Christmas, continuing on throughout the spring. The waiting is the hardest part.

Lunch time. Friday. The day of the Regional Championship. The bond between acquaintances is temporal at best but true friendship weathers many a storm. After witnessing the cruelty Mason allowed himself to be party to, Talley realized her friendship with Page was worth more than being a shadow for a swell-headed jock. With their friendship on the mend, Talley began to confide in Page once again. Though she was not a pauper by any stretch of the imagination, Talley swore Page to secrecy after telling her of her parents' decision that she work nights to help pay for her college education. "Can you see me waitressing at a pancake house, Page? How humiliating!" "I think that's the point your parents are trying to make. Heaven forbid Bianca even considers requiring me to do menial labor. I'd sooner go to California and live with my father, wicked stepmother and sister!" As an after thought, Page remembered her college was already allotted for in a trust fund. "I hope this is just a temporary arrangement, punishment for dating that slime Mason. My mom said she had never been so embarrassed in her life. Me being brought home in a police cruiser, even if it wasn't my doing that put me in that situation." Talley was about to find out her secret wasn't as secret as she thought.

Chyna Nance was gorgeous. Four-feet eleven inches tall. A ninety-pound waif – stunning gray eyes and facial lines so perfect that if she stood still long enough she could be a mannequin. Mason sought her out after he and Talley broke up in order to keep his reputation from being sullied. Chyna and her clique called themselves the Revlons, a projection of their aspirations to become models. They were well-versed in the rumors of the lifestyle many models lead in order to keep their Covergirl figures. Its difficult growing up in the Nineties with all the various special interests groups campaigning for rights, and the freedom to be who they want or think they want to be. She and Mason talked about her inner turmoil. Last night, Thursday, they ate at the pancake house on Buchanan and Taft. Talley didn't see them because her tables were on the other side of the restaurant; but they recognized her as she repeatedly approached the grill to retrieve her customers' orders. Maybe she was ignoring them. Why else would Talley have a job that kept her up so late near Buchanan Forest when she lived in Crystal Springs.

Chyna sauntered over to the table where Page and Talley sat, trading stories of how gross Mason Cole was. She leaned behind Page ever so deliberately, allowing her breast to touch Page's back. "Mason told me you like girls. I'm curious to know how true that is." Chyna then looked across the table at Talley and laughed. "By the way, you look nice in that checkered dress and apron." Page couldn't decide which upset her the most, the indignity Chyna had bathed Talley in or the sickening feeling of Chyna's breast lingering on her back. "You're just as ignorant and confused as that idiot Mason if you believe that. And as for Talley," Page began before she realized she was yelling, pulled Chyna close to her, "Where and when she works is her business!" Chyna waited for Page to loosen her grip on her sweater, and then suddenly kissed her just in front of her ear leaving shimmering blue lip prints on her cheek. "Everybody has a secret, girlfriend," Chyna laughed mockingly. In the end, Page had the last laugh. She went to the principal and lodged the last in a number of complaints that had been lodged against the different members of the Revlons, which ultimately led to Chyna receiving a ten-day suspension for sexual harassment.

DAVENPORT BRIDGE

Crenshaw and Bradford were separated by a tributary that was approximately one-quarter-mile wide. In the early Fifties, both towns sprang up in support of the thriving peanut industry. More specifically; a large peanut-butter company. Just as rivers separate land masses, they historically served as the border for racial polarization. Crenshaws' northwest corridor, home for the more affluent black families, was connected to Bradford by parallel train and road bridges, which served as the main supply route for the factory which lay in the northeast corridor of Bradford. Civil rights and desegregation came along with expansion, both industrial and metropolitan. Initially, as with all hints of change, there was great resistance. The good people of Bradford fought vehemently against the ruination of their piece of Heaven, emanating from the westward migration of Negroes. The eventual merger, then buy-out of the peanut-butter factory with a much larger candy conglomerate,

59

heightened racial tension, leaving in its wake an innocent casualty of ignorance.

Tyler Beaumont and Thomas Charles Davenport Jr. (T.C.) were best friends-blood brothers. As a matter of fact, they were still sporting flesh tone Band-aids on their pointer fingers. They were as best of friends as a black and white boy could be in 1969. The Davenports were the first black family to cross the tracks into Bradford. T.C. Davenport Sr. was a company man, a graduate of Tuskegee, who could have been born of the very sweat of George Washington Carver himself. Anyway, one day Tyler and Little T.C. were running from their sisters, attempting to lose them, so they could play on the old abandoned train bridge. Eventually, the boys eluded their sisters by ducking behind a bush. A bush Tyler remembers today even though he begged his father to burn it down the day after the horrible thing happened.

T.C. and Tyler didn't see the group of cherry faced teenagers in various stages of undress preparing to dive into the pond hidden beyond the weeping willow trees. They never knew Everett Sumner's father was beaten out for a management position by Thomas C. Davenport Sr., solely on the merit of his knowledge. Affirmative action had not come to Bradford yet. They didn't even know who Everett Sumner was until he and his gang pounced on them. One boy held Tyler in a Full Nelson and four or five others carried T.C. onto the train bridge, kicking and screaming. When they were half way across the bridge they put T.C. down. "Get on your own side of the track, Nigga' boy. That's where you belong. My dad says a educated nigger is too smart for his own good!" You could hear a chorus of "yeah, that's right!" from the gallery. "But I live over there," T.C. pleaded. "Let him go," Tyler cried, struggling to free himself from the freckled faced behemoth that held him in the seemingly inescapable hold. "I said, get boy, and you better run!" T.C. started running toward the Crenshaw end of the bridge, then suddenly, turned back toward Bradford and Everett Sumner. Everett could not believe the little shine's defiance. As T.C. bore bullishly toward him, intent on getting to this rightful home, Everett stepped aside and tripped him. "You're going the wrong way, Sambo!" The thud T.C.'s head made when he struck the track was deadeningly fatal. He was dead even before the group of boys pushed him off the bridge into the water. "Run. Everybody run!," Everett shouted. Tyler stood there in awe. Shock set in so quickly it took all the strength his sister, Missy, and T.C.'s sister, Bertha, had to pull him from the spot where he stood and coax him into running home with them to tell what happened.

Everett Sumner got a good lawyer. Justice was blind to the facts, but not to the money in 1969. Tyler swore his friend would not be forgotten. On December 1, 1984, after fifteen years of lobbying by the Beaumont family, friends and supporters, the old train bridge was renamed for Thomas C. Davenport Jr. and turned into a bike path. It would have been T.C.'s twenty fifth-birthday. The corner stone read, "In memory of Thomas Charles (T.C.) Davenport Jr. He dreamed of becoming an astronaut. Here's to what could have been."

Over the years, Bertha would go stand under the street lamp at the Bradford entrance to the bridge and stare at the spot where the police pulled her beloved brother from the water. She would stand solemnly for five minutes, offering a prayer to God for either another brother or a son who looked like him. Then she would wade knee deep into the water and set a handful of daisies adrift with the current. With the exception of Bertha's private vigil, the area near the bridge, especially beyond the willow trees, remained the same. The seclusion of the willows was the spot where many young ladies lost their innocence.

Eric Prater never met his uncle T.C. but he figured he had to be all that if his mother loved him so much. Tonight, December 1, 1994 he stood with his mother, knee deep in cold water, thanking God for the son who had grown to look like her brother. "You know, you were conceived under that bridge over there. Your daddy and I were sitting, watching the stars and the lights sparkling on the water, and ..." "Okay Momma, I know you loved Uncle Thomas so much that you went against Grand Dad's wishes and got with Pops. Love you but, this water is getting cold. Are you ready to go now?" Then the eeriest thing happened. A chill ran up his body to his head, then out his fingers, leaving him standing there, fingers tingling. Was it the night air or was it Uncle T.C.? Either way, it was spooky enough. "Momma, I'm outta here. I'll see you in the car!" "Place this rose in the water for me before you go, Baby. Give me another two minutes, okay?" "Okay."

Eric hurried to the car and dried his feet. His hands were still tingling when he remembered the football sitting in the rear window – it was the game of the season when he single-handedly beat Morristown kicking five field goals. Score 15-14. For some strange reason, he felt compelled to place it at the base of the corner stone honoring his Uncle T.C. Two weeks passed before he noticed it was again resting in the rear window of his mother's car. Bertha purchased another ball, placing it at the base of the bridge instead. "Momma, when did you put this ball back in the window?" "The day after you left it on the bridge; mothers know the things their sons cherish. It was the thought that counts, Sweetheart!"

CHANGE OF HEART?

Pooh's plan to humiliate Chenelle at the slumber party fell through for the obvious reason - Chenelle was hangin' with her crew that night. In her heart of hearts she didn't really want to team up with Chelsea anyway. One of the articles she read in Essence, discussing how valuable friendship is, highlighted how life is funny at times and how fickle youth can be. Chelsea would have to devise her own plan to get revenge on Chenelle.

As fate would have it, Beth Minor tore a ligament in her right knee doing a somersault/split during the regional game, leaving the squad with only eleven cheerleaders to cheer during the quarterfinal game and possibly beyond. It is the state custom that the last three rounds of play-offs; the quarter, semi, and State Championship games be played in the Dome. Due to the awe and splendor associated with playing in the Dome, it would be a travesty not to have a full complement of twelve girls on the squad during the game (s).

Opportunity knocks. Sunday morning. Chelsea sat at the breakfast table with Morgan, her 13 year old sister, who was also captain of her cheerleading squad. Although she was a Pop Warner cheerleader, she believed her status in the city youth football circle was just as prestigious, and took her job just as serious as Chelsea did. "So Chells, what are you going to do now?" "It's not my decision Moe, it's up to Ms. Lamay," Chelsea sighed. She reached into her lap to give Samantha, her Calico, a piece of biscuit. Samantha was a mite too aggressive when she bit into the fluffy biscuit catching the tip of Chelsea's finger with her razor-like teeth. Startled, but not really hurt, Chelsea's reaction was unexpected and definitely out of character – she thanked Samantha! "What are you thanking the cat for, Weirdo?, any other time you would be screaming at her and threatening to have her stuffed." "Yea, it's weird, but I just got an idea. I need to call Ms. Lamay." Chelsea left the kitchen and went upstairs to her bedroom to put her plan into action. She called Ms. Lamay and explained all the reasons it was the best solution to their problem to offer Chenelle the opportunity of a lifetime – cheering in the Dome just like the professionals. What better way to finish your high school career. "I have no problem with it. Call Chenelle and we'll all talk with the principal and athletic department tomorrow to make sure it's legal. Have a good day." Chelsea was elated. Now, to get Chenelle to take the bait.

Nona was putting the finishing touches on the Sunday meal while everyone else changed into their hang-around clothes. When the phone rang she thought it was Mother Brown calling to ask why she didn't sing this morning. "Mother Brown I..." "Mrs. Henderson, this is Chelsea McDavid. Is Chenelle there?" "I'm sorry, baby, I thought you were my choir director. I'll get her for you." "Thank you," Chelsea responded, hearing Mrs. Henderson call Chenelle to the phone.

Chenelle had pretty much made up her mind to take advantage of the opportunity to cheer once again, wearing purple and gold, but she had to round table it with her girls first. It was too exciting to wait until this evening before YPWW to talk with them, so she called them and asked them to meet her at Davenport Bridge. "I think you should do it, girl. The band is going to have a slammin' routine and you know the majorettes costumes are going to be the bomb!," Cookie announced, barely able to contain her enthusiasm. "Yeah, girl, and 'Roni and I are going to be clowning in the stands. You know we gotta show those mountain people the Marshall Strut!," 'Tonya added. Finally, as a postscript, 'Roni proclaimed, "It's gonna be on girl. It's no guarantee we're going to state so we better get down to the Dome while we can." "Okay then, I'll call Chelsea and tell her I'll do it. I just hope I don't have to be her roommate. All she'll want to do is talk about Jarad." "I don't blame her sister, you brother is…," 'Tonya laughed, tracing an outline of Jarad's phantom body in the air. "Don't go there Miss 'Thing'. Chelsea will claw your eyes out if she knew you were lusting after her man," Chenelle teased. "Don't forget about Jacques either, girl," Cookie said, tracing an outline of his body as if to remind LaTonya of the gift she had. They sat around for about another half hour teasing the squirrels and ducks before going home to eat the meals their mothers had prepared.

The week that followed was a frenzy of bake sales, candy sales, and various other fundraisers. Each of the student auxiliary clubs solicited donations from civic organizations and local businesses to aid in paying for the additional buses which were needed to transport those students who wanted to be at the event of the year, playing in The Dome. Once all the funds were collected, drivers contracted and student consent forms turned in, the dreaded teacher, parent and alumni chaperones were identified. Freedom, as they say, comes with a price.

THE TRIP

The four buses set aside for carrying the football team, band, cheerleaders and majorettes, left Bradford Friday after school to ensure that each group would not be road weary and, therefore well rested for their quarter-final game which was scheduled to begin at 12:00 Noon, Saturday. This also allowed time for site seeing Friday evening. The eight additional buses, carrying the devout and adventurous members of the student body, did not leave Bradford until Saturday morning at 6:00 Am enroute to the state capitol – a five hour trip with traffic, four without. This would allow for anyone interested to visit the sights around The DOME before the game started, since the after-game itinerary was to return to Bradford as soon as possible so as not to be charged additional rental fees for the buses.

Chenelle's worst fear was confirmed when Miss Lamay read the list of rooms and roommates to the girls when they were about an hour outside of Bradford. Even after she and Cookie pleaded with Miss Lamay and Mrs. Pace, the Majorettes' director, Miss Lamay remained adamant about keeping her cheerleaders today. Cookie was so angry with Miss Lamay's decision that she continued to plead her case with Mrs. Pace until the director finally offered her star lieutenant some consolation by telling her, "Andrea, if I had the last word to say about this, Chenelle would be one of the three girls sharing the room with you, but it's not my decision to make. We have to respect Miss Lamay's reasoning and get our minds focused on majorette business now. Okay?" "Well, at least we can sit together while we're traveling," Cookie conceded, walking back to the seat she and Chenelle shared two rows behind the driver. Her elbow, "accidentally," found the back of Chelsea's head as she passed her seat on the aisle. Although it was no more than a slight tap, Chelsea's "Ow," countered by Cookies' "What?!," prompted Mrs. Pace to warn, "Okay Miss Tisdale, I'm watching you!" "You better slow your roll before you get us both in trouble, Cookie," Chenelle cautioned. "I'm gonna be hangin' out in your room until they call lights out anyway, so chill. Okay?" "Okay!!!"

Upon reaching the capitol, the four buses from Bradford pulled into the Morrison's cafeteria just down the street from the motel where they would be staying. Cookie sought out Malcolm and Eric and invited them to share their table, "since they (coaches and directors) don't mind if we eat together," she said snidely. "It's messed up that everybody won't be here until tomorrow," Malcolm stated. "Yea, we could be having a lot of fun," Eric continued. "Why do they call you 'Foots'?" "Why do they call you 'Cookie'?" "I asked you first!" "I asked you second," Eric teased. "Anyway!," Cookie pouted angrily. Seeing Cookie was upset, Eric slid his size twelve foot from beneath the table and pointed toward the floor. "They've been this big since the seventh grade." "I'm sorry Eric. That 'Thing' over there," pointing at Chelsea, "is on my last nerve. My brother was teasing me when I was in kindergarten, so I threw an Oreo at him." After that, whenever I got mad, everybody would say 'watch out for the cookie girl.' The Cookie part stuck."

The table was quiet for a few seconds before Cookie spoke again. "I wonder what they're talking about," once again looking over at the table where Chelsea now sat with Damon. "Fleas are always attracted to dogs," Foots and Malcolm laughed, slapping five across the table. "What's so funny?," Kenyan interrupted, approaching Chenelles' table, with 'Tange in tow. "Be gone little boy!" "We havin' one of those days, Cookie?" "It's Andrea to you, runt. You know I don't allow freshmen around me, shoo!" "You gonna let her dis' your little brother like that 'Nel?," Kenyan asked jokingly. "She's not having a good day, Kenny, so you and 'Tange need to go on over there with your band friends, okay?" "I don't know who..." Tangela started, "and you don't want to know either, girlfriend, so don't go there!" "Kenny!" "Okay, 'Nel, I'm out but she needs to stop trippin'." After Kenyan and Tangela were gone, Eric looked over at Cookie as if he were her father or mentor saying, "True dat 'Drea, you need to hold your temper a little better than that. They didn't do anything to you. I hope Malik does something to fix that at the game tomorrow." "What's that suppose to mean?" "Whatever," Foots answered before pulling Malcolm by the shoulder. "I'm gone man!" "We'll see you guys at the hotel, okay?," Chenelle said apologetically. Later that night, Cookie apologized to everybody for allowing 'that thing' to upset her so much. If she only knew what Chelsea and Damon had planned, she'd know that the funny feeling she had in her stomach was friendly intuition at work, that he animosity for Chelsea was justified.

True to plan, Chenelle hung out with Cookie and her roommates playing spades until lights out. Tea Brant and Tiesha Waller were at the mall. Ever so carefully, Chelsea rummaged through Chenelles' belongings while she had the room to herself. When she found what she was looking for, she called Damon and arranged to meet him by the swimming pool. "I have a present for you, Big Boy," she announced enticingly. "I'm there!, Damon responded, anxiously hoping she had what they'd talked about at the restaurant. The die was partially cast. Chenelle unwittingly anted in a bonus chip when Ms. Lamay observed her talking to Damon by the vending machines. "Young lady, it's two minutes until bed check, and you Mister, I don't have to tell you what Coach Hawk would do if I told him you were down here talking to one of my girls, do I?!" "I'm out Miss Lamay, you know I don't want no more trouble with Coach." Then, as he turned to leave, he intentionally dropped a note at Chenelles' feet and bounded up the stairs barely able to mask the Cheshire grin on his face. GAME/SET. Hopefully, MATCH would come after Mr. Henderson received an anonymous phone call.

Although Chenelle had no intentions of picking up the note, it appeared to Miss Lamay that the lovebirds were attempting to make her look silly. "Don't touch that note Chenelle," she directed. "On second thought, bring it to me!" "I didn't plan to pick it up anyway. I ain't tryin' to hear anything Damon has to say. I was just coming to get some sodas for me and Chelsea.!" "Yeah, and I just fell off the bread truck, too. Go to your room and we'll deal with this tomorrow after the game!" "Whatever," Chenelle mumbled dejectedly; suddenly realizing she had been played.

THE GAME

The Dome opened its doors at 8:00 AM in preparation for the series of play-off games to be played throughout the day. At 8:30 AM the press box began announcing the schedule of events. A few cheers rang out from the sparse crowd. It was too early to be up on a Saturday if your team wasn't playing. Fortunately, Marshall was scheduled to play against Jackson county Mountaineers during the second contest of the day beginning at 11:00 AM. In spite of the schedule, the Panther contingent would find out there was "…no such animal as too early" during the play-offs.

Coach Hawk held an 8:00 AM wake up call and instructed his players to be on the bus at 8:30 AM. Breakfast at IHOP. Unbeknownst to Coach Hawk, the Mountaineers had chosen the same spot for breakfast; however, one half hour earlier. The 'mind' games began as soon as the Panthers entered the breakfast haunt. Demonseed and Spawn were the first in line behind Coach Knight, the Defensive Back coach. Ashley

Cannon, the Mountaineers' All-State Offensive Guard, recognized the tandem immediately. "Hey, you two look smaller in person than you do on film. Oh yeah, allow me to introduce myself, Ashley Cannon, the next great right guard to play for Clemson before being drafted by the Raiders as the glue for their offensive line. Oh yes, I'm a bad man!" "Talk to the hand Gomer," Spawn started in before Coach Knight pulled his collar and directed him to the tables the waitress was pointing out. "Save your talk for the game, Mr. Cole. Right now you need to concentrate on breakfast!" Ashley wasn't through with his harangue. "Edwards, the cat got your tongue or does your coach have his hand up your back too?" This brought a roar from the rest of the Mountaineer players who were filing out of the restaurant. Damon spun around and spouted; "Demonseed and Spawn, #95 and #91, that's all you need to know fat boy!" "Now, now, is that anyway to talk to a future teammate? I heard Clemson had their eyes on you too. It would be an honor to play with you for four years of college, that is, if the Raiders don't come for me before I graduate." "Hey Coach, come get your boy before I let my dogs get him right here," Coach Knight shouted, himself tiring of Cannon's tirade. Spawn looked at Coach Knight in disbelief saying, "And you just told me to chill, how you sound?" "And I'll say it again, shut up and focus on what you and your shadow have to do today. The boy is as bad as he thinks he is. I just don't want him to get into your head before you suit up. Can you feel that Mister?" "We're here Coach," Mason motioned pointing from his eyes to the coach's' and then back to his again.

The Marshall student, parents and fans began filtering into The Dome at 10:30 AM, anticipating the game of the year. This game between Marshall and Jackson was billed as the game from which the eventual State Champions would emerge. Everyone shared the same hope that their trip from Bradford would reward them with the victory necessary to advance to the next step enroute to winning the Class AAAA Championship title. The thunderous sound emanating from the entrance of the tunnel alerted the fans to the impending arrival of the High Stepping Panthers of Marshall High. The football team came roaring out of the tunnel to the beat of the band and the majorettes chanting, "Go head Panthers, strut that stuff, ahh, STRUT THAT STUFF!" Damon, Eric and Toby Washbish, the quarterback, were the three captains Coach Hawk sent out to the center of the field for the coin toss. Marshall loss the toss and elected to kick from the south end of the field. The Mountaineers had three captains, also. Of course, Ashley Cannon was their mouthpiece. "This is going to be fun," he said reaching out to shake Damon's hand. Damon snarled and slapped Ashley's hand to the side before turning back toward the Panther's sidelines and flashing the kick-off sign to Coach Hawk. "Put your foot into that thing Prater," Coach Hawk encouraged his kicker as his Panthers took the field. The tat-a-tat-tat of the snare followed by the timberous roll of the tenor drums and finally the simultaneous boom of the bass and clash of the cymbals signaled the start of the game.

The Hendersons and Tisdales found a spot behind the Marshall bench as close to the 50 yard line as possible. The student body had filled most of the seats below the tenth row just beneath the band and majorettes who had rows 11 -19, seats #6 -20 cordoned off. This left seats #1 – 5 and # 21 – 25 open. The Praters and the Tates were two rows above the Hendersons and Tisdales. Many other parents and family members found seats as best they could in the mob of Marshall students who were fortunate enough to make the trip. "Hey, Miss Nona, how you?," came the playful voice of 'Roni with 'Tonya at her side. Close behind them were Malik, Jacques and Kadeem. "Hey baby, are you guys behavin' yourselves? I don't want to take any bad reports back to Bradford with me." "Of course we are, Mrs. Henderson. The chaperones and teachers are threatening suspension for anybody deciding to cut up on this trip," Jacques sighed. "How is your wrist young man?," Micah queried taking Kadeem by surprise. "I'm fine sir. The therapist has me doing range of motion exercises to build strength." Kadeem's tentative response helped the Hendersons realize the awkwardness he felt speaking to them when he still hadn't sat down and talked with Chenelle except in passing, since that day in the park. "Kadeem," Nona started before Micah squeezed her wrist. "Let it go baby, the kids have to work this out themselves." "I was only going to ask him if he would like to come to dinner tomorrow night."

"It's okay, Mr. Henderson, I was planning to talk to Chenelle at half-time and apologize for being so distant. If Chenelle doesn't mind I'll be there. Thanks for the invitation." "Are you happy now Mother Busybody?," Micah teased, nudging Nona in the ribs. "Come on ya'll, we need to let these old people enjoy the game," 'Tonya laughed. "You're a mess girl," Mrs. Tisdale laughed back. "He is a handsome boy, Nona. As usual, Chenelle found a good one. It's a shame that Edwards boy has forgotten where he came from though." 'Roni and company were already out of earshot so they didn't hear Mrs. Tisdale's lament. She couldn't be more correct. Damon wasn't through spinning his web.

The Panthers and Mountaineers played their game with a degree of ferocity akin to the classic feuds between the Hattfields and McCoys. For the first two quarters, each serial drive down field was thwarted by the defensive team. Each offense had to settle for a pair of field goals in the first quarter. With a minute left in the second quarter, Marshall kicked another field goal. They led the (9-6) at half-time. "Hey fat boy, when are you and the rest of your hayseeds gonna start playing some football?" "I didn't see you city boys cross the goal line, did you? I think we're doing our job as good as you are. I ain't heard the fat lady sing yet either!"

After the bands completed their half-time routines and the cheerleaders exchanged cordialities, Chenelle went into the stands to visit with her parents for a few minutes – to warn them that Miss Lamay might call them after the game or after their return to Bradford. "We'll deal with that when and if the time comes, Babygirl. You go back down there and cheer the best you ever have until now." "Thank you Daddy, you always say the right things." She kissed her parents, caught up with her crew, then returned to chastise her momma for meddling in her business. "Roni and 'Tonya told me you asked Kadeem over for dinner tomorrow. Momma, why didn't you talk to me first; how am I going to grow up if you don't let me handle my business my way?" "If your daddy had said something to him we wouldn't be having this discussion, would we, Miss Lady. I just thought somebody needed to be sensible about this thing. I saw the note you left on the dining room table Thursday night. You want me to tell you what it said?" "No momma, you don't need to go there. I just wish you would have asked me first." "I'm sorry Baby, it's just a mothers curse to be nosy." When Micah slapped her thigh, Nona looked up to see Kadeem standing behind Chenelle. "Speaking of the Devil, I think you two might have something to talk about!" In the few minutes left before the second half kick-off, the couple apologized to each other for not initiating this talk before an adult brought them to their senses.

Malcolm ran the kick-off back 73 yards for a touchdown shocking everyone, himself included. His longest run before today was a hard earned 35 yards when he played Pop Warner ball. The Mountaineers made a bad gamble when attempting to go to their limited passing game. Spawn intercepted the pass and advanced an additional fifteen yards. His heads-up play resulted in another touchdown run by Malcolm. The Panthers had raised the score and thus the stakes in the first five minutes of the third quarter. Score 23-6

After hearing Marshall's crowd sing "This is how we do it!," twice in five minutes, the Mountaineers decided enough was enough. "If we're going to beat these guys we've got to pull our heads out of our butt, our tails from between our legs and make this dog hunt!" And hunt they did. All the clichés the Mountaineers' coaches could use to motivate their players were pulled out of the collective hat. The first was, "Slow and steady wins the race, we're gonna run that ball off tackle until they get sick of seeing this formation." For three consecutive series the Mountaineers ran from the POWER I set, third man carrying the ball. Each time the end result was to punt and prepare to play defense. Marshall's offense could do no better. They couldn't even get inside the 30 which was Foots' maximum range for a field goal. "If at first you don't succeed, try, try, again."

The Panthers punted after failing to get into field goal range. They didn't expect the Mountaineers to do anything fancy, at least fancy for the Mountaineers. Foots punted the ball deep into the left side of the field to the Mountaineers 15 yard. Stanley James Holcomb, the Mountaineers back up Tight End, caught the ball and ran toward the right hash mark as fast as he could with the Marshall Panthers coverage team in hot pursuit. Every one of the Panthers' cover men committed the one cardinal sin every special teams coach preaches against. "Stay in your lanes," Coach Williams warned, but no one listened. No one noticed the wall forming back on the left side of the field until it was too late. Stanley James Holcomb spun in his tracks and threw a spiraling screen pass to Amos Cotton, alias Junebug, which would have made Joe Montana envious.

"Get him Edwards," was the last thing Damon remembered before he opened his eyes to see Chenelle standing over him asking if he was okay. He had taken the right angle of pursuit. Junebug should have been stopped at the Mountaineers' 15 yard line. He would have been stopped had it not been for the critical block #63 put on Damon. He never saw Ashley Cannon barreling down field leading the Mountaineers drive to score. Cannon reached down to help Damon to his feet. "Not a bad hit for a boy named Ashley, huh Demonseed?!" "F@#K you, Hayseed!" "Let's not get personal Bro, it's just a game. A man's game that is!," Ashley punctuated his taunt before the referee pointed him toward the Mountaineers sidelines. "Get your head back in the game Edwards, we've still got a lot of time to play and I can't have you getting into a grudge match with that ox. We warned you he was good!" Coach Hawk didn't let on to the fact his stomach flipped when he saw his defensive star flying toward the cheerleaders, propelled by the velocity of Cannon's blindsiding him. Damon would have time to get the cobwebs out during the point after try (P.A.T.) and the ensuing Panther offensive series. Score 23 -13.

Chenelle granted Chelsea another caveat. When seeing Damon lying at her feet, she fell to her knees, almost hysterically, pleading for him to get up and let everyone see he was okay. As he and Coach Knight walked back to the bench, she unconsciously kissed him on the cheek while patting him on the butt and assuring him, "I knew they couldn't keep you down. You go boy!" All in the bounds of cheerleading, but not everyone saw it that way, especially Shayla and Kadeem. The picture Gina took of Chenelle's innocent action only served to fuel the ire of the green eyed monster. It would be another two days, Monday, before she again saw it in "The Paper Panther" during lunch. The headline read: "Homecoming Queen gives Demonseed a boost of confidence in losing effort during quarterfinal game. Score 23 -30." The quarterfinal play-off was over but the 'games' were yet to be.

Monday afternoon. Amidst the small talk at the beauty salon, Pinkie (Sarah) Hines was heard expressing her concern about her baby's possible sexual activity. "Red, I think Shay and Damon have gone and got themselves in trouble. She usually comes to me when she starts cramping and asks me to make her a warm milk toddy, but she didn't come to me this month or last month and it's almost Christmas. She's two months overdue!" "Girl, I hope you're wrong. That Edwards boy is nothing but trouble!" Pinkie wouldn't know for sure that her daughter was intimately involved with Damon until Pooh burst into the salon, laughing hysterically. "Momma, you wouldn't believe what happened today outside of English class!" "Pooh, can't you see I have a shop full of women waiting to have their hair done. Tell me about it when we get home, okay baby?" "Red, you need to let that baby go 'head and tell what she knows," Florence Jordan interjected. Her daughter, Chereth, was in Shayla's Physical Education class. "My Cherry been telling' me that Shayla ain't been dressing out for P.E. for the last month. To make it worst girl, she told me that little girl threw up on the bus on the way back from that game Saturday. Go 'head Pooh, tell your momma what you know!" "Flo, I'm not trying to let my daughter become a gossip monger like you," Red began in a feeble attempt to save Pinkie and Sharon Edwards, sitting two chairs away having her hair washed, the embarrassment of having their business in the street. "Pooh, I said we'll talk about it at home!" "I don't see why you tryin' to be so hush mouth about it Red, everybody knows that boy ain't nothing but trouble." "Florence Jordan, if I don't want my baby to be rude and disrespectful, it's my right. If you're trying to start some mess in my salon then you can leave." "You ain't the only beautician in the neighborhood sista, you charge too much anyway!" "Don't let the door hit you where the good Lord split you, ole hussy!" Red sighed aloud acknowledging the $35.00 dollars she'd just lost, a sigh that brought relief only twenty minutes later. "Thank you for trying to spare my feelings Red," Sharon began. "But if this gossip is truly about Damon then I would like and need to know. Here's the money for Flo's hair and my shampoo. Tell me, what happened at school today, Pooh?," she continued calmly. Pooh looked at her mother for approval. "Go 'head girl, the damage has already been done. Here honey, take your money back. Florence isn't worth all this fuss." "It's not about Flo or the money Red, it's the principal of this thing," Sharon said thinking how much she sounded like her husband. Then she turned to again to Pooh. "Shayla and Damon were arguing when I came out of the bathroom. When I got closer, she slapped him and started yelling about how she didn't get her period and how could he let Chenelle pat him on his, excuse me Momma, but she said 'ass,' when she was going to have his baby!" "Is that all that happened Gina," Sharon asked in a more parental tone. "Hold on sista, it's not POOH you're mad at," Red interjected protectively. "I'm sorry baby; it's that boy and his irresponsibility that's starting to get to me." "Damon called her a lying Skeezer and pushed but she got in a kick and scratched him on his cheek before a couple of the football players started pulling him down the hallway." "Thank you Pooh," Sharon offered in frustration. Then she picked up her tote and left the beauty salon after placing the money for her shampoo and what Florence would have paid for her weave on the cash register. "It's going to be a long Christmas Red." "You're right girl, you're truly right."

Thinking about all the trouble Damon had already been in, Red looked over at her daughter and chided, "I told you it's not always good to tell what you know, Gina. I can call you that, I'm your momma!," she continued emphatically, to the frown Pooh wore on her face. "That woman's been through enough with that boy this year without you adding to it. If it's not your mouth, it's that camera!" "I wasn't trying to start any mess Momma, I was just doing my job. I didn't tell her to lay up under Damon." "Watch your mouth Gina. You still live under my roof and eat food that I buy. You just need to be a little more careful baby is all I'm trying to say." "Whatever," Pooh whispered to herself while walking into the back room to begin her homework. "It's all Chenelle's fault." Although Red heard Pooh's snide remark, she knew it was an act of acquiescence rather than disrespect that prompted it.

BLESSING IN DISGUISE

The telephones were abuzz Monday evening with the gossip spurred on by the lovers' spat between Shayla and Damon. The two mothers spoke and agreed to wait until the children brought them into the picture or, better yet, give them until New Years Eve to tell the truth about their "problem." "We don't need to tell their fathers, girl, especially Graylin, he'll kill your son. He wanted to beat him up after that thing at Mason Park. I know it takes two and you cant' tell a young girl she's not in love when she's fifteen going on thirty, but you have to convince Damon that manhood isn't between his legs!" "I know Pinkie, I know. You be sure to tell me if and when she gets her period. We don't have much time to get this fixed if she is pregnant!; I 'm not ready to be a grandmother." "Neither am I, but we have to give Shayla a chance to make her own decisions." "I'm not in total agreement with you on that but as a woman I can see that being her right. Let's just pray we don't have to cross that bridge."

Two weeks passed before anything substantial happened. With the threat of suspension hanging over his head, Damon kept his distance from Shayla. This only served to infuriate her more and elevate the level of jealousy and contempt she had for Chenelle. Miss Lamay asked Chenelle to remain on the cheerleading squad up to the first day of Christmas break. During half-time of the girls' varsity game, Shayla threw a NOW-N-LATER candy at 'Tonya as she walked over to the referee to hand him the ball, striking her in the shoulder, 'Tonya immediately darted toward the stands, but Chenelle cut her off before she reached the edge of the court. "Let it go 'Tonya, she's trying to get at me through you." "I ain't the one Shay. Throw something else and not even your punk boyfriend will be able to keep me offa you!" When Shayla stood to respond to 'Tonya's threat, she fainted, slumping into Chereth's lap, who herself became hysterical. The Hines were called and informed that Shayla was being transported to Bradford Memorial. The decision was made, due to the information Chereth gave Coach Chitwood (Head Basketball Coach/Assistant Principal) concerning the altercation in the hall last week.

"Mam, the EMT said she kept saying, 'I'm going to lose my baby...,' over and over again. We were afraid to give her any medication or perform any testing prior to your arrival. As a matter of policy, she being a minor, with the exception of a truly life-threatening injury, your consent to perform more definitive testing is required. Right now our presumptive diagnosis is she's suffered a bout of vertigo or syncope. Do you think she's pregnant, Mrs. Hines?" "I don't know Doctor, but it is possible. She usually comes to me when she's cramping but she hasn't done that in the last two months. I was talking with her boyfriends' mother hoping it's not too late to consider..." "We have to be sure there's a pregnancy before we start considering alternate courses of action, Mam." From the slight inflection of his voice, Mrs. Hines understood his moral stance even in this professional arena. For the next two hours Shayla was subjected to a series of lab tests and a pelvic exam which yielded hopeful yet paradoxical results. While the lab tests were 99% negative for pregnancy, the doctor felt a mass where her right ovary should have been. "I don't care what he says, Momma, I AM pregnant with Damon's baby. A lot of women don't start to show until they're four of five months along!" "Miss Hines, both the testing performed with your urine and blood sample...negative for the presence of Human Chorionic Gonadotrophin (HCG), the hormone that is excreted during pregnancy." "I ain't tryin' to hear that Doctor. Come on Momma, I'm ready to go home!" "Mrs. Hines, she needs to schedule an ultrasound to rule out various other possibilities." "Look, Mister, I told you I'm pregnant, I don't need no test to prove that, you'll see next month!" "I'll give you a call in the morning Doctor, she's not going to agree to anything right now." "You do that, Mam. She doesn't know what she could be doing to herself!" "I'm going to the car, Momma!" "Okay Baby, I'm coming, I just have another question for the doctor. Could Shay be suffering an hysterical pregnancy?" "Pseudocyesis? Well, yes but I'm more inclined to believe she may have the beginning of a cyst or possibly an ectopic pregnancy." "She is so obsessed with Damon that she's convinced herself a baby will keep him. I'll have he Daddy talk to her so that she'll agree to have the test done next week!" "Thank you, Mrs. Hines. Your wisdom at this juncture could be the difference in you eventually becoming a grandmother or never at all!" "Thank you, Doctor O'Han-ra-han?," Sarah sighed quizzically. "O'Hanrahan is correct, Mrs. Hines. You've done better than most. My medical school buddies just called me Alphabet. Do be sure to have Shayla schedule that ultrasound. Goodnight."

Sarah found Shayla standing next to the driver's side of their smoke grey Cressida, arms folded as though she were readying herself for an argument. Mother Wit told her to be patient, but Shayla's antics in the emergency room coupled with the apparent defiant posture were wearing on her patience. When Shayla demanded the keys, Sarah decided it was time to put the sisters, Patience and Prudence, to bed and let her know who was in charge. "Get in the car Shay, I'm through fooling with you tonight!" "And?" "And you should be happy I didn't slap you in the mouth for being so disrespectful in the emergency room. I was giving you the benefit of the doubt because of your hysterics!" "Hysterics? Momma, please, a woman knows when she's pregnant!" "How is it that you CHILDREN say it now days, 'Slow your roll?' Well, I think

that's what you better do. Fifteen does not grown make…!"
Shayla yanked the passenger door open, slumped into the
seat and slammed the door leaving Sarah in mid sentence.
Sarah walked around to the drivers' side and got in. Shayla
turned and began to look out the window. "You can look out
that window all you want little girl but you are going to hear
this! How many times have you been with that boy?!," Sarah
demanded, not really concerned with the exact number. She
was merely setting the stage to make her point. "His name is
Damon, Momma, not that boy! Three times since the night
before Halloween." "That's my point Shay. Although some
girls get caught on their first or second time, it rarely happens
that way. More times than not, women or girls, feel guilty
about what they've done or they want to keep their man,
and I say that very carefully, so badly that they hope they
are pregnant." "That's not my problem, Momma!," Shayla
answered raising her voice ever so slightly. "Raise your voice
again sister and I'm going to remind you of how much of
a woman you're not. You've gotten on my last nerve. I'm
through with it. You better hope your daddy doesn't kill you
and that boy!" She looked over at Shayla sitting with her arms
crossed, pouting like the confused fifteen-year old that she
was. "I can't keep coming to the rescue like this Shay. Your
daddy is definitely tired of Damon! I'm going to schedule
that ultra-sound for next week if you don't get your period
soon and that's the last thing I'm going to say about this!"

Shayla continued to frump (pout) even as they drove into their driveway. Graylin was sitting in the living room when he noticed the beam from the headlights racing up the foyer walls and was at the door when his wife and youngest child entered. Thinking she had reached solace, Shayla reached out crying, "Daddy, it's not my fault!" "What's not her fault Pinkie?" "She thinks she's pregnant by Damon." Before anyone could utter another word Graylin had Shayla by her shoulders shouting, "What?!" "The doctor felt a mass near her right ovary but all the lab tests he did for pregnancy were negative. It's probably a cyst but there is a small chance that it would be an ectopic pregnancy." "So why don't we know?" "She refused to have an ultrasound done because she just knows she's pregnant!," Sarah answered sarcastically. "He also agreed that it could be an hysterical pregnancy!" "It better not be any kind of pregnancy if you know what's good for you and that boy young lady. I asked you about this mess when I picked you up from the dance and also at the park, Shay!" "I told her if she didn't get her period this week…" "I don't care about her period. She better not be pregnant or I'm going to have that nig…," then he caught himself. Graylin hated to hear a black man call another black person such a denigrating name. He couldn't understand why the young people thought it so cool or acceptable to address each other that way. "I'll have him put in jail for statutory rape!" "You can't do that Daddy, I wanted to be with him!" Sarah and Shayla both screamed when they heard the resonance of Graylins' open

90

palm slapping the wall – causing Shayla's second grade picture to crash onto the floor. "Monday, Pinkie, Monday, you will take her to your doctor and have the ultrasound done. God help me to keep my head until then!" "I'm sorry, Daddy," came a feeble utterance from Shayla. "Go to bed Shay. Pray God sends some angels to hover over your bed and to watch over young Mr. Edwards until you come from the doctor's office on Monday. I'm not going to let some thug wanna'be ruin your life!" Shayla knew there was nothing else to be said to her father. Knowing her mother was right all the time, she wisely cut her losses and apologized before kissing Pinkie good night and adjourning to her room.

Pinkie and Graylin talked about their options should Shayla be pregnant in spite of all the tests, or at least Pinkie did. Graylin was firm in his stand that Shayla would not have a child at fifteen years old. "Enough of this, babies having babies. I don't see many of those right-to-life advocates rushing to adopt the babies they're pushing people to have, especially little black ones!" "You sound like Sharon has been talking to you Graylin!," Pinkie protested angrily. "And when did you talk to her Pinkie?" "Last week at the beauty salon when Pooh...," Pinkie froze in mid-sentence. "When Pooh what, Sarah?" "When Pooh come into the salon talking about the talk going around school." "And?" "Just girl talk Gray, gossip."

Sunday came and went in a hush. The Edwards kept their distance, even though the only conversation between the two families was the talk Pinkie and Sharon had at the beauty shop. Shayla's absence from P.E. Monday started rumors anew and by lunch time the cafeteria was abuzz with speculations of Damon and Shayla's pending parenthood. By the end of the day however, all rumors and speculations were proved to be wrong. The results of the ultrasound concluded that Shayla had a cyst involving her right ovary. Her surgery was scheduled to take place during Christmas vacation in order to save as many absentee days as possible.

The surgery went well, but youth being an evil, spiteful and fickle beast, refused to let a sleeping dog lie. Chereth Jordan, of all people, kept the rumor alive that Shayla had had an abortion.

THE PARTIES

You couldn't count how many Christmas parties, dances and birthday parties there were during the two week hiatus, not even if you wanted to. As a result of those parties, however, many new bonds were formed and many friendships were strained. One such bond which was born was that of Chenelle and Page, due to their mutual disdain for the Salt and Pepper tandem of Demonseed and Spawn.

Christmas Eve Page celebrated her 17th birthday. Though she would have preferred the festivities to carry on late into the night, she had to settle for the 7-9:00 PM time slot at the Chamberlain Commons club house. The later hours were reserved for the mature set to hold their soirees. Bianca took the liberty to submit a guest list of twenty people which included a few members of the student council, a few civilized jocks and, finally, Kadeem and Chenelle.

"You know I only accepted the invitation so I could get a head start on my extra credit project. Besides, me and Kadeem are talking again. A sister has to protect her interest so I don't see why you're giving me attitude." "I don't have a 'tude Chenelle," Cookie continued, "I'm just teasing. Now you just gw'on up to Chamberlain Crossing and do us proud!" "You are definitely a twisted sister 'Drea. You know you're my girl thru thick and thin." Cookie reached out and pinched her bestest friend on the cheek before walking away. "And don't you forget it either, Chenelle." "We'll see you at T.J.'s girl. I'm sure you and Malik will find something to keep you busy until we get there," Chenelle laughed. "Don't go there Sista, I'm not even curious about doin' that thang!" "You can say that again Cookie. Hey, did you get a chance to call Shayla?" "The sister hung up after she told me any friend of yours wasn't a friend of hers. Damon's got her mind child!" "I feel sorry for her but she won't accept my calls either. Anyway, I gotta get ready before Kadeem gets here. See you at the real party." "Okay," Cookie agreed before hanging up.

When Kadeem and Chenelle entered the clubhouse they had no problem separating the student council types from the jocks, the snobs and the glad to be heres. Page worked the room feverishly encouraging the groups to mingle. Chenelle watched admiringly, remembering the poise Page displayed at the Halloween party despite the betrayal of her best friend. After ten frantic minutes of failure, Page finally conceded and allowed the hostess Bianca hired to earn her pay. Page was now free to mingle with her guests as recklessly as a teenager should. She sat down to collect herself as that tiny maternal voice in her head repeated, "Page dear, you take yourself too seriously; enjoy your youth while you can!" This was truly a hard task be it she had no siblings to entertain and a mother who refused to be an adult.

"I hope you two are enjoying yourselves." "It's working for an uptown girl," Chenelle chimed. "You sure know how to work a room, girl." "I had a lot of practice watching my mother, especially before my parents got divorced." Sensing a mood swing, Kadeem quickly changed the subject. "I see you and Talley are friends again. Isn't that her by the punch bowl with Brent?" "Yea, she saw Mason for the creep he was. Speaking of creeps Chenelle, that was a crazy picture of you patting Damon on the butt in the school paper!" "Embarrassing is a better word, I can't believe Gina put her out there like that!," Kadeem interjected. "I told you Pooh apologized for taking that picture. She wasn't trying to start anything, it's her job. Matter of fact…" "I know you told me she begged Ms. Walker not to use it. I'm still trying to figure out how the Bradford Sentinel got it?" "If you look at the pictures again stupid, you can see they're from different angles. The one in the city paper isn't Pooh's!" "Damon is milking that picture for all he can though. I'm getting tired of him throwing it up in my face. Always the same thing, 'If you were handling your business, your girl wouldn't be tryin' to get up on this man sized booty!" "I keep telling you Damon is the biggest Buster I know too, Kadeem. YOU are the person I'm with, okay?!" "Okay!," Kadeem agreed. "Sorry, I didn't mean to start a fight here people." "It's me Page. Every time I make a fist I remember the dance, the day in the park and now this picture. Damon is everywhere!" "That's probably why they call him Demonseed," Page offered jokingly. "Evil is always around when he's near!" The teens laughed at the face and crossing motion Page made around them as if to ward off that evil.. Evil that was still afoot unfortunately. The house party at T.J.'s would deliver a present Chenelle didn't need.

Mother Graham reluctantly agreed to allow T.J. to have a party at her house if he agreed to his Aunt Gloria and Uncle Terrance being chaperones. T.J. agreed with the quickness of Mercury. "Yeah, they're not old heads like Mom and Pops!" Anyway, the party was flowing smoothly when Chenelle and Kadeem arrived. Kenny and Tange' were standing on the wall in the kitchen just happy to be hangin'. Chenelle looked over at the Christmas tree which reminded her that everyone was supposed to bring a neutral gift to exchange. "Kadeem, we forgot to bring the presents in." "Oh snap, I'll go back to the car and get them." Off he went. Chenelle circled the room looking for her girls. When she heard Roni's shrill laughter, she knew they were in the backyard. Not only did she find Roni, Cookie and 'Tonya but Pooh was with them too. Back in the fold.

M.C. Hammer's latest hit was pumping when Kadeem came back inside. He put the presents under the tree, motioned inquisitively toward Malik and Jacques who himself hunched his shoulders signaling he didn't know where the girls were either. Malcolm knew. He'd been outside talking with a few of the other neighborhood boys and came in to go to the bathroom. Taking Kadeem by the ear and motioning to Jacques and Malik, he led the trio outside to the girls. "Okay ya'll let's set this party off," Malcolm shouted pulling Roni away from the group. Everyone else followed suit. Eric Prater asked Pooh if she wanted to dance. "Okay, Foots, but don't put those boats on these little feets of mine," she laughed. "Oh, you got down with that one Sister but I ain't mad at ya!" The scattered chorus of "Where's the party at?," "Right here!," echoed throughout the house and yard. Then the ugliness started.

It would be silly to expect Damon to behave with some degree of civility even in the face of all the trouble he could be in. If Shayla had an abortion it wasn't his problem. Who knows who else she'd been with. His parents never approached him about the baby so everything must be chill, right? Wrong. He just ducked the blow. Anyway, the sudden silence that took over the house when Damon walked in with Chereth could be heard by the deaf. Little Miss Cherry strutted through the living room and out onto the patio with a look on her face that dared anyone to say anything to her. Damon was her man now. It wasn't her fault Shayla got pregnant. It wasn't her fault Shayla's parents forbade her from seeing Damon anymore. No one said anything – not right away.

Damon's focus went right to the redheaded girl standing by the refrigerator talking to T.J. "Hey Red, I know I'm slumming comin' back to the neighborhood but you are definitely a long way from home aren't you?" The young lady just looked and rolled her eyes at his rudeness. "Didn't Bae Ruth show you enough at school Damon?" "This ain't your business T.J. Didn't I show you enough in the woods?!" "That was ten years ago my brother!" "And this is now. I'll take you and Red outside and break both of you up. What's with this Bae Ruth stuff anyway? I thought her name was Heike!" "Heike stood beside T.J. taking his hand into hers. "My name IS Heike to you Buster but to my cousin and the rest of my family it's Bae Ruth!" She practically dragged T.J. across the room to the fireplace. She snatched the picture resting on the mantle pieced of Mother Graham holding hands with a little white girl standing next to the Berlin Wall. Six additional wallet sized poses surrounded the 8 x 10 photo of the two. One of those pictures was Heike at eight years old standing in the very living room where they stood, wearing a pair of her father's blue jeans – her hair corn-rowed, adorned with beads. "I have more right to be in this house than anyone other than T.J." "Save the Drama for your mama, Red, I ain't tryin' to hear that noise. You know you're in the wrong neighborhood. And then you're trying to prove to everyone how black you are by coming in here wearing China knots in your hair!" "You can dis' my hair all you want Damon, at least it's real. You're just jealous because you can't get with anybody that' older than fifteen. And then you gotta get a skeezer who stabs her best friend in the back." Chereth started to speak but Chenelle cut her off. "Don't go there Cherry, you did enough damage spreading those rumors about Shay having an abortion!" "Why are you always in my business Chenelle?," Damon countered. "Oh yea, this is for you!," he laughed tossing a small package at her. Kadeem caught it. "Good catch sucker. It's the panties she left in my room while we were at the Play-offs!" Chenelle's inner circle knew it was a lie. The question was how he got them.

Aunt Gloria stood at the entrance to the hallway observing the whole exchange. Terrance stood behind her. When Damon announced the contents of the box she told Terrance to make him leave. Terrance, who was a mechanic, had no problem ushering the demon seed to the door and down the block to his Tracker. Chenelle looked at Cookie and burst into tears. It was possible a pair of her panties were in the box. She couldn't find the black cat pair when they returned from State. She figured they'd been misplaced or lost. Now here, Damon plays her in front of the whole neighborhood. It really didn't matter what was in the box. Damon gave everyone something to talk about. Kadeem would probably trip on the way home so 'Tonya and Cookie walked with Chenelle.

Although Kadeem didn't trip, he was flustered. He knew it was probably best that the girls walked Chenelle home.

It was only a five minute walk around the corner. "Why is Damon so gone over Chenelle," Kadeem asked anyone who would answer. T.J. was the only one who spoke. "He's been that way since we were in the second grade. Ever since the Tom Thumb wedding we acted in at church." "Is that it?," Kadeem asked in disbelief. T.J. knew there was more but didn't feel it was his place to tell it. He did, however, tell Kadeem of an incident that let him know he wasn't the only person Damon hurt because of Chenelle.

"When we were in the fourth grade, Skipper Green, the center from Taft, lived right down the block. Anyway, he liked Chenelle just as much as Damon did. Since he was a little bigger than the rest of us he wasn't intimidated by Damon." "Okay, so?" "So," T.J. continued, "Damon had to stay after school for talking during library period. Skipper asked Chenelle if he could walk with her and the girls." Pooh was listening to the story from the doorway. She began feeling guilty for her part in that day's near catastrophe.

"On the way to school that morning Randy told me he liked me. He even gave me his Chips Ahoy cookies at lunch. Well, when he asked Chenelle if he could hold her hand, I was furious. I ran back to school and told Damon they were holding hands. I didn't think he would do anything crazy, I just thought he would give him a bloody nose or black eye like he did everybody else!" "So what did he do that was so bad," Kadeem demanded. "I mean neither of those compares to a broken arm and dislocated wrist!" "Everybody knew Randy was allergic to ants but we didn't understand they could kill him, not at nine years old anyway. We just knew he needed a shot if he got stung by one. After Damon got home he poured some ants down Randy's back." Pooh now in tears, T.J. finished the story. "If I hadn't ran to tell Skippers' moms, he would have died. All Damon said was, 'Ants in your pants makes you dance,' then he ran home." "That's a sick brother," Kadeem scowled. "Even though he was probably thinking the shot was the worst pain Skipper would endure."

Kadeem mentally exhausted. Damon is definitely Demonseed. With Chenelle gone, he bid T.J. good night before giving the room a shout out. "Merry Christmas everybody, I'm out. Peace!" Then he walked over to Pooh to offer a consoling word. "It wasn't your fault. Who knew the brother was going to grow up to be as stupid as he was then?" "Yeah maybe, but it's not Chenelle's fault either. I should never have told Chelsea I was mad with Chenelle also. Merry Christmas Kadeem," Pooh offered dejectedly. "Merry Christmas Pooh, it's all good." The two teens hugged briefly. Kadeem left the party. Pooh asked Foots to drive her home shortly after that.

Micah was doing his usual thing when Cookie knocked on the door. He wondered who could be knocking at the door on Christmas Eve. Nona was in the den tying the last bow on Sade's ears. "Hey Cookie; why aren't you at the party with the rest of the kids?" "Because that idiot Damon just ruined it for Chenelle. He dissed her in front of everybody. She's at Roni's 'cause she doesn't want you to hear her crying!" "Nona, you need to go to the Sapp's and bring my Babygirl home," Micah spoke calmly, trying to mask his anger. He had to let Chenelle grow up, to have those growing pains. "Come on Cookie," Nona directed. "Lets go manage this crisis. 'Nelle needs to stop letting that boy get to her." "Miss Nona, you don't understand. Every time it seems like Chenelle and Kadeem are getting closer, Damon throws some mess in the way!" "Listen Baby, I know you're her best friend and I'm her mother, but we can't protect her always. There are going to be other boys and men in her life after Kadeem. You are still too young to be so serious." Knowing Miss Nona's words were true, Cookie was seething nonetheless. By the time they reached 'Roni's however, she and Miss Nona were laughing at Sade, chasing a frog.

Carmen Sapp answered the door nibbling a pieced of her special Harvey Wall Banger cake. "Girl, what are we going to do with these ladies? Chenelle is upstairs with 'Roni. They need to do something with Damon. That boy's not going to be happy until somebody hurts him. I was happy when Linford bought that house in Killian Woods!" "Thanks Carmie let me go up here and get my child." "Can I get you something to drink Andrea? I have some of your favorite iced tea in the kitchen." "No thanks, Miss Carmen." "How about some of this cake?" Cookie didn't pass on the cake.

She could satisfy her sweet tooth and get a slight buzz on too. She liked the Wall Banger cake better than her mother's rum cake. Missionary Tisdale only let her sample a small piece every Christmas.

Nona waited patiently as Chenelle washed her face and made a feeble attempt to pull herself together. After mother and daughter left the Sapp's, arm in arm, 'Roni and Cookie walked back to the Graham's. T.J. told them he and Pooh had told Kadeem about the day Skipper almost died and how it upset Pooh again. "She asked Foots to take her home but Bae Ruth talked her into staying. They're out on the gazebo." 'Roni, always the clown, took it upon herself to save the day one more time. She got their mind off the past by cracking a few jokes about the football trip. This in-turn triggered memories of the bus ride and the restaurant and Chenelle telling them about the note.

The note Damon dropped in front of Ms. Lamay asking Chenelle to meet him after lights out. "For Chenelle to meet Damon, she would have to leave her room, right?," 'Roni surmised. "Right!," Pooh agreed. "She was in my room most of the night," Cookie chimed. "Didn't she tell us Chelsea asked her to go to the coke machine?," 'Tonya queried. Then it hit them. "That B@#*@!," Cookie screamed. "She set her up. I knew it. She took Chenelle's panties when she was in my room and gave them to Damon!" "We ought to kick her butt!," 'Tonya proposed. "You know if this hadn't happened to 'Nelle it would be funny!" Cookie laughed agreeing with 'Tonya. "It is funny. But it did happen to our girl so, I'm going to step to Chelsea just for that. You with me?" "It's on sista," the girls agreed. "We'll get her on different days, accidentally of course." They made their secret sign and went back inside to enjoy the party. Merry Christmas.

A MOTHERS' LOVE

Christmas Day passed without a word of what transpired at T.J.'s party. This was truly surprising. Mother Graham rarely let something like that pass without offering her opinion about fast little girls. No, she didn't speak on that until New Years Eve before Watch Night service began.

"Nona, I don't know if you know what happened at my house Christmas Eve but you need to talk to your daughter about striking matches without having a bucket of water handy." "What are you saying, Mother Graham?" "I don't need her teaching Bae Ruth any bad habits. Glo told me she had Terrence put that Damon out of my house because he told everyone the gift he brought to the party was a pair of your daughter's under-garments!" Mother Graham paused deliberately before firing her last shot of admonition. "If you had talked to her when she got in trouble in the woods years ago…" "Okay Mother Graham, you've made your point!," Nona said calmly though visibly shaken.

The girls were sitting in the choir loft listening to Heike's tale of how Mother Graham came to nickname her Bae Ruth. "It's from that story in the Bible. Remember Ruth stayed with Naomi even after she told Ruth she was free to go back to her people? Well, when Grandmother was sick, my moms came from Germany and took better care of her than my aunt Gloria and the rest of my dad's brothers and sisters did. If my mom was Ruth, then I had to be Baby Ruth or Bae Ruth." "I remember that," 'Roni shouted. "You were the little girl that came with the nurse." "That's right. My father's unit was on a mission at that time so he told Mom to come check on Grandmother." "Why didn't T.J. tell us you were his cousin then?," 'Tonya asked. "Because he didn't think a white lady could be his aunt back then. You know children think." "What about when you moved to Bradford last year?," Cookie interjected. "Why didn't you tell it then?" "Because Grandmother didn't think it was necessary." "She didn't think it was necessary?," Cookie continued. "Your grandmother is a trip, Heike. Always in your business but doesn't want you to know hers!" "You're so right Cookie," the girls agreed. "It's a miracle she hasn't busted Chenelle out yet!," Pooh commented as an after thought. Heike offered one last consoling word. "I guess she means well though. Having nine children, she doesn't know how to be anything but the neighborhood mother!" She looked over at Chenelle, wondering why she hadn't yet joined in the conversation. When the door to the sanctuary opened, she figured it out.

Not a word was spoken when Nona walked into the sanctuary. Her affect was so foreboding, Chenelle knew Mother Graham had been biding her time. The girls could see the hurt on her face. She hurt for her Babygirl. She hurt for herself. "Why couldn't you tell me yourself?" Chenelle tried to say, "I don't know," but the words would not come. She thought, "How could you understand the anguish I'm going through." No, there hadn't been a physical assault or consensual anything. It was mental. It was Damons' sick game. She didn't know what to say but she hoped it would get back to her mother through the grapevine, via Mother Graham. Nona just walked to the altar. Chenelle met her there. A few moments later the rest of the congregation began filtering in. The pastor spoke on shedding the old and putting on the new. "God Bless us all in 1995, Church. God bless us all. Amen Amen.

While they were praying, Nona remembered Chenelle warned her and Micah that Ms. Lamay might call them concerning her alleged behavior. She squeezed her daughters' hand as they stepped onto the crowded porch. As they descended the brick steps she said, "I would have believed you Babygirl." "Thank you, Momma." The Lord works in mysterious ways.

The New Year was here, time to return to school. The girls' varsity basketball team had a game the first day back. 'Tonya couldn't stay focused during physics. All she could think about was the dynamic duo from Taft, Annette Wallace and Nia Bell, wizards of the backcourt. Both handled the ball equally as well as they shot. "I'm going to get it going and coming," she thought aloud. "All right Miss Walker, you don't want to be the reason three people fail this test do you?!" Knowing this to be a rhetorical question, she continued marking answers arbitrarily. There'd be other tests. Hopefully, she'd fare better during the game.

The dread from the test carried over into the game. The first half was pretty even all around. Defensively, 'Tonya got help from Becky Whitten, ponytail swishing through the air. 'Tonya's ball handling and assists, as always, was the mainstay of the Lady Panthers game. The forwards were keeping the ball on the glass and the center regulating the middle. The second half was a disaster. Taft came out for the third quarter with the fury of Diana. Ready for battle. They trapped. They zoned. 'Tonya was so frustrated she didn't care when Coach Stanz sat her on the bench for five minutes. When she put her back in the game, 'Tonya's' apathy was infectious. "Time out!," Coach signaled. "If you don't want to act like my team captain Miss Walker, I'll sit you on that bench so long you'll need a whoopee cushion. Now you take this team back on the court and play with some fire!" 'Tonya looked at her coach so hard that if she was Medusa, well, you get the point.

The dynamic duo picked up on 'Tonya's frustration quickly. Trapping her at half-court on the inbound pass, they forced her to commit a back-court violation. Frustration turned into recklessness. She didn't hear Becky's numerous warnings to "watch out for the pick" ending up on her butt half a dozen times. The final insult came when she tried to shake Nia only to bang knees with Annette, allowing Nia to strip the dribble and proceed down court for a lay-up. As with all clichés, Insult is married to Injury. 'Tonya's collision with Annette propelled her to the hardwood, leaving her with a thigh burn and a hyper-extended wrist compounded by a greenstick fracture of the 5th metacarpal bone (between the pinky and wrist) on the left hand. (Boxer's fracture). What a night!"

Sore and embarrassed after her on-court mishap, 'Tonya opted to miss school the next morning thereby missing a ride in the "Max." Mother and daughter Tisdale worked a deal on driving the Maxima to school. Chenelle initiated the morning conversation by turning to 'Roni saying, "Girl, I don't know about all these people getting their wrist broke all of a sudden. All the wrecks we had on our bicycles when we were little – the worst thing any body got was a busted lip!" "I know girl, first Kadeem an now 'Tonya. I wonder who's next?" "I don't know but I hope it's me!," Cookie teased. "Maybe then Malik wouldn't clown so much when I ask him to carry my books!" "Girl you're stoopid, you've been watching too many movies!," 'Roni chided. "Don't forget to remind Pooh its' her turn to accidentally bump into Chelsea." "What?, Chenelle asked in surprise. "I know you three haven't been bothering that girl!" "Oh yes we have. That thing didn't have to do what she did to you!" "And what was that Cookie?," Chenelle demanded. "We figured she gave your panties to Damon while you were in Cookies' room during the play-offs," 'Tonya declared.

Chenelle spun around, pulled the sun visor down and began brushings her hair angrily. When she looked into the vanity mirror she saw 'Roni making faces at her. She was trying to be mad. "I ain't tryin' to see you Veronica." "Why?" "Because a sista's got a right to be mad when she wants to!" "Well, we're not going to let you," Cookie laughed poking Chenelle in the side. "You know it would be funny if it wasn't you it happened to!" Chenelle looked at Cookie then 'Roni, and the three began to laugh. And laugh. And laugh. When the hysteria subsided, Cookie continued. "But since you're our girl we can't let her think she got away with dissin' you like that. We decided, the four of us, to make her life miserable for a while!" "And you're getting her back for what happened on the bus too, admit it Cookie," Chenelle added. She looked at her friends and just shook her head, thankful for the years from second grade until now.

If the girls' bond was stronger than steel, then the mothers' friendship was definitely amicable. Carmen called each of them and invited the group to meet her for lunch. They agreed to meet a Zula's Fish Fry about two blocks from Davenport Bridge. "Great, I need to run by the house any way to check on Rufus and 'Tonya," Monique Walker announced. "I'll see you and the rest at Zula's." Carmen, Nona, Red and Victoria Tisdale sat down in the booth over-looking the pier in the bend of the river. The topic at hand was their daughters were soon to be mature women, off to see the world in a few months. Although college was the dream of the parents, nothing was yet etched in stone.

"Ladies, the girls are practically grown now. We need to have some idea what their plans are so we can try to help them out." "Pooh has a promising career in photography, girl, at least an apprenticeship at the newspaper." "Chenelle is talking about law." "And as much as I dislike it, Andrea is applying to the School of Performing Arts. She wants to dance professionally!" "Well," Carmen sighed, trying to hide her embarrassment, "It seems as though you sisters have done your homework. 'Roni wants to be a track star and a child advocate." "I know," Nona acknowledged. "Chenelle told me Wilma Rudolph is her idol." "That's right. She doesn't know it yet but I wrote this letter to Tennessee State to make sure they know my baby wants to come to their school." The letter was placed in the center of the table for the mothers to see. Red picked it up and began to read:

Carmen Sapp
25 Lena Horne Dr.
Bradford, wherever

Tennessee State University
3500 John A. Merritt Blvd.
Gentry Center 307
Nashville, TN 37209
ATTN: Track Dept.

To Whom It May Concern:

I'm writing this letter on behalf of my daughter, Veronica DaChelle Sapp, who is a stand-out track star at Thurgood Marshall High School, Bradford, Wherever. Ever since watching the Wilma Rudolph Story she's been fascinated with Track & Field and the dream of becoming an Olympian just as Ms. Rudolph did. Except for facing the childhood adversities of her heroine, Veronica is just as swift and graceful.

I don't know if her coaches are aware of her dream to become a Tiger Bell, trained by the legendary Coach Temple, but I am determined to ensure my child has the opportunity to realize her dream. Aside from athletics, she plans to major in Early Childhood Development.

Please write her with all the information she needs to make herself eligible for a scholarship at Tennessee State University. She is already a Tiger Bell in spirit. Thank you.

Sincerely,

Mrs. Carmen A. Sapp

"That's a nice letter Carmen," Victoria began before Zula approached the table announcing Monique Walker was on the phone. "Did she say what she wanted?" "Something about you coming to her house to pray for Rufus." "Rufus?," Carmen asked in disbelief. "Yes, Rufus. She said she got home only to find her daughter in the back yard crying over Rufus. Who is this Rufus anyway?" "You don't really want to know," Carmen continued. "Well shouldn't someone call 911?," Zula asked confused by everyone's lack of concern. "Rufus is their dog!," Red blurted. "You know some people think of their pets as family," Zula said. Her statement was not profound in and of itself but it did provoke the group of mothers to remember how long Rufus had been in the Walker family . Twelve years. Two years longer than the average life span for a German Shepherd.

No one answered the door when Missionary Tisdale rang the bell. Due to the circumstances, she entered the home calling to Monique while continuing toward the kitchen. "We're in the back yard," Monique answered. "Baby, please let him go. He's gone." "Not until she prays for him Momma!" Conventional wisdom would suggest Missionary Tisdale be real with 'Tonya – telling her animals don't have souls. Mother's love won out. While 'Tonya knelt crying, Rufus's head cradled in her lap, Missionary Tisdale recited a few verses from the third chapter of Ecclesiastes. When she finished she placed her hands over 'Tonya's. "He's at rest now Dear. Why don't you go inside and lay down. I'm sure your mother will do what's best for Rufus. God bless you Dear." Amidst her tears 'Tonya uttered a weak yet sincere, "Thank you Missionary Tisdale." She kissed Rufus's cold snout and said goodbye.

After 'Tonya was inside, Missionary Tisdale looked at Monique quizzically. "I heard her screaming – pleading with Rufus to wake-up when I came through the door. She knew he was gone but she wasn't going to leave him without you praying over him." "I only prayed for her sake Monique." "And I thank you. 'Tonya does too. Matter-o-fact, like you , I believe she really wanted you to pray for her strength in dealing with losing Rufus and the chance to finish her basketball career at Marshall High. The doctor said it's going to be -8 weeks before her hand heals." "You remind her, the Lord puts no more on us than we can stand. I'll tell Nona and the rest about this when I get back to Zula's, okay?" "Thank you, Victoria. I need to call Bernard (Mr. Walker) and have him call the veterinarian."

Bernard went by the vets' to settle Rufus's account on the way home. He turned onto Lena Horne Drive passing Veronica, Pooh, Chenelle and Cookie – walking from the Tisdale's. "How are you ladies this evening?" "Fine, Mr. Walker. We came to see how 'Tonya is doing," Pooh answered. "I don't know if she's up to having company. I just came from the vets'. Rufus left us this morning." "Was he sick?" "No, Pooh, just old. Twelve years is a pretty good life for a German Shepherd. Come in, I'll see if she's up to seeing you." 'Tonya was ready for company. She was also fighting mad.

Cookie was first to reach out to 'Tonya offering her condolences. Her hug was received without reciprocation. Watching 'Tonya's refusal to embrace Cookie left Chenelle, 'Roni and Pooh disheartened. Her venomous outburst was like a dagger. "Save the drama Andrea. I don't need YOUR sympathy. You only came because of Chenelle!" Cookie stood awestruck, wondering what prompted this attack. "You know you never liked Rufus. I don't know why you came!" "Your father just told us about Rufus outside," Chenelle offered. "It was Cookie's idea to come see how you were doing girlfriend," 'Roni added. Then Cookie spoke. "I thought we were better than that." "Better that what? You told me yourself that you liked Chenelle and VER-ON-I-CA better than you liked me. Everybody knows you were afraid of Rufus!" "That was second grade 'Tonya." "And this is now!," 'Tonya shouted. The tears began welling in Cookie's eyes. "Come on," 'Roni said. "She doesn't want friends right now,

she want s to fight. You can't argue if we're not here sista!"
"Get out then. I'm a big girl!"

The door slammed, confirming 'Tonya wanted her friends to share her pain, but not the way they intended to. Bernard entered the foyer to find her glaring at the door. "Where are the girls, Muffin?" "I kicked them out and stop calling me Muffin. I'm not a little girl anymore!" "Is this about a nickname or something else?" "Well she didn't have to come here pretending she felt sorry for me!" "This isn't about Cookie. It's not her fault. He's gone, Muffin, but your friends aren't. A woman would realize that and make it right!"

Muffin lumbered into the kitchen, poured herself a glass of ice water, then pouted her way passed her father into her room. She knew her was right but in her mind she had a right to be mad. Pop Pop, her paternal grandfather, gave Rufus to her as birthday present when they visited the country. "I think a pretty little six year like you should have him," she remembered Pop Pop saying. "I promise to take care of him until I'm a hundred years old!" We all know babies have no clue about time.

The phone rang while she lay slumped over her purple futon couch, wondering how to make amends with Cookie. It was Pooh. "'Tonya, I just wanted to tell you I know how you feel. I didn't loose my dog but do you know how long I was jealous of you guys for having a whole family, how much I hated you, Chenelle and Cookie for being the center of all the attention, especially at church?!" Pooh continued to talk about the numerous articles she read in Essence extolling the virtues of friendship and how God predestined everyone's life. She talked until she convinced 'Tonya that Chenelle didn't seek out popularity, it came to her. Cookie was just always there at her right hand. "Some people just have that charisma. You can see some of Chenelle's charm has rubbed off on Cookie by how concerned she was when you missed school today. Look, I got three-way party line. Why don't you let me call Cookie so you two can talk this thing out?" 'Tonya remembered how her father had said, "Tonya would realize...", then picked up the inference of his calling her Muffin. It really wasn't about a name – it was about maturity – about friendship. Pooh made the connection, 'Tonya and Cookie talked, the friendship was mended – LaTonya was born.

January trudged on. All was going well for the Fab 5 until, one morning, during homeroom, each of them received a notice to come to the dean's office. All were equally confused when they met in the hallway joining the cafeteria and the administrative wing. "What's going on?," Chenelle queried. "Your guess is as good as mine sista," Cookie answered. 'Roni took the liberty of opening the office door. When they saw Chelsea sitting next to the secretary, it became crystal clear.

"Please have a seat ladies!," the dean directed. "I'm a little distraught to hear of the allegations Miss McDavid is waging against you. I find it hard to believe the five of you would risk five days suspension for harassing her over God knows what?" "What have we done?," Cookie answered coyly. The dean looked at Chelsea, observing her body language. He then noticed the intensity of Cookies' stare. "Chelsea tells me that she's had a 'pushing encounter' with each of you at least once since school reconvened." "She must be imagining things Sir because I don't have any classes with or near hers!," Cookie snapped. "Chill Cookie, she has to prove everything she said," 'Tonya added. "I talked with Miss Lamay. She told me of the incident you had on the trip to state, Andrea, which lends some credibility to Chelsea's story." "Ask her what she did to Chenelle, go ahead, ask her!," Cookie demanded. 'Roni and 'Tonya grabbed her, stopping her from closing the distance between herself and Chelsea. "I didn't do anything," Chelsea quivered, a ploy exaggerating her fear.

Cookie was her own worst enemy. Chenelle fueled her anger by saying, "We can't prove anything either!" "Tell him Chenelle," Cookie pleaded. "Why are you letting her play us like this?" "Chill Cookie," 'Roni warned. She realized the dean now had enough circumstantial evidence, against Cookie at least, because of her present actions. "Settle down Miss Tisdale. Seeing how animated you are, I'm going to send everyone else back to class. After you calm down, I'll allow you to explain why you feel Miss McDavid deserved you harassment." Cookie looked at her friends filing out of the office. "I thought we were tighter than that!" Friendship is fickle but it is true.

The dean didn't make Cookie elaborate after she prefaced he statement with, "This is very embarrassing for Chenelle." He did, however, put two and two together, surmising there had been some bad blood between the triad. The other girls were drawn in due to loyalty. Miss Lamay told him about the note. As far as he could see, the only real harm was done to their individual egos. "I'm willing to let the issue die with a verbal warning. I can't see any good in punishing the homecoming queen, cheerleading captain, dance squad lieutenant, newspaper photographer and the rest over such sophomoric pettiness!" Even after acknowledging how embarrassing the revelation would have been to Chenelle, Cookie felt betrayed. As far as she was concerned, Chenelle let Chelsea win again – at Cookie's expense. She decided she wouldn't speak to Chenelle for two weeks.

WHO WOULD HAVE GUESSED?
(VIGNETTES)

There were nearly 100 pairs interested in the extra-credit project - Sixty-five percent girls, thirty-five percent boys. Very few of these pairs actually needed the credit but Mrs. Fulbright's hard sell speech convinced many that it was a means of preparing them for the world beyond Bradford, be it college, the military or community life as an adult.

At his mother's urging, Kadeem invited Mason Cole to be his partner. Neither youth knew it was actually one of the conditions their fathers agreed upon as a means of "healing the wounds" from the dog attack. "Dude, I freaked when I heard your bones crack. I didn't know Damon was that whack." "I didn't either. Fortunately, I'm left handed so it didn't hurt as much, mentally that is!" They found their similarities to be:

1) their birthday – July 23rd

2) their fathers were lawyers – however different sides of the table

3) they each had one sibling – a younger sister

4) they liked baggy clothes and,

5) they both played three tiered chess.

Their differences; the first was obvious:

1) Race – Kadeem was black, Mason , white

2) Haircuts – conservative fade, ponytail

3) Compact car, truck

4) Kadeem was following dad into law, Mason wanted to be an Entomologist.

Kadeem was just as awestruck by Mason's bug collection as Mason was impressed with Kadeem's knowledge of classic court battles. "Dude, I couldn't tell you the difference between a tort and a tart." "Well, I was lost after you showed me the difference between a beetle and a boll weevil." They talked about the similarities between Chenelle and Page. Mason confided how he'd realized he was wrong to pit Page against Talley. "All three of them are class Dude. I was just trying to prove to everyone I wasn't a geek." "We're still young brother, with a lot of mistakes to make." "You're right," Mason agreed, "but I'm learning a lot from talking to Chyna." "Isn't she the one who got suspended for kissing Page?" "Yeah. I can't tell you her business but I know she's not a lesbian. She's just confused."

Malik and Malcolm both lived in Flippers Valley, named for Lt. Henry O. Flipper, a Buffalo Soldier. However, everyone knew the best place to get a fresh cut was at Langford's Barbershop in East Crenshaw. Malik was in the chair when Malcolm came into the shop laughing. "Yo, yo, yo, Malik, guess what I just saw in Pizza Hut?" "What?" "I saw your girl with Chyna!" "And?" "I was trippin'. She got suspended for tryin' to get with blondie so why is she tryin' to press up on that brown sugar tip?" "Why you wanna act like a buster man? You know she's doing that extra-credit thing!" "'Tonya told me Cookie hasn't talked to Chenelle for a week and a half. What's up?" "It ain't na'than (nothing). She's still trippin' on that panties thing Damon pulled at T.J.'s party. She said Chenelle and her crew dissed her when the dean called them to his office." "Yea, she has been acting a little whack G!" "You better get somewhere Malcolm before it ain't na'than between my foot and your @*s except leather and denim. You're going where you don't need to go!" "Ain't no need to flex my brother. I was just having a little fun - my bad." "We here," Malcolm sighed apologetically. Some jokes are a little too close for comfort.

At Pizza Hut, the conversation between Andrea and Chyna was very similar to Malcolm and Malik's. Chyna confided that her curiosity was borne out of the accidental revelation that her aunt's best friend was really her lover. It was hard for her to fathom why two gorgeous women didn't have male companions. Her aunt's answers were equivocal at best. She did, however, make it plain that it was a choice and not genetic. "My aunt Jenny is the coolest. I guess that' why I'm so confused at times. I think Mason Cole is a dream come true. The bad thing is, we like the same person." Cookie looked puzzled. "You don't need to ask if that is why I got suspended." "I heard that rumor. Have you read Romans?" "What's that?!" "It's a book in the Bible." "I'm agnostic!" "What's that?" "I need more proof of the Omnipotent God!"

Chyna's last comment caused Andrea to sigh aloud which sent Chyna into a short tirade. Time to play Devil's Advocate. "People use the Bible to repress your right to explore what's natural! You have the right to feel good however you choose!" "Romans, sister - you need to read Romans!" Chyna turned up the heat. She wanted to see how strong Cookies' convictions were. "I think you're hiding your real feelings for Chenelle behind that Christian facade!" "Don't go there Chyna!" "Why?; because it might be true?" "How you gonna front me like that?!" "I mean, why else would you blow-up so quickly when someone insults Chenelle or gets to be closer to her than you are?!" "Because she's my best friend!" "I think it's because you want her to be more than that!," Chyna laughed. "That's why you're going to hell, Chyna!" "Why don't you just tell me to go to hell?" "Because I'm better than that! I knew I made a mistake picking you for my partner. I'm out Chyna and you're lost!" "No, I'm confused!," Chyna laughed once again. Then hammering the final nail into the coffin, she added, "Oh yeah, 'judge not lest you be judged'."

Sometimes laughter is the best medicine. This wasn't one of those times. Cookie was appalled that Chyna would dare to suggest she harbored Sapphic feelings for Chenelle. Chyna was upset with herself for trying to ease her pain by hoping Andrea would question her own orientation. The saving grace was their strongest similarity. Neither had ventured beyond casual petting or a French kiss. VIRGINS. EIGHTEEN. CONFUSED. Both would eventually do the "right thing." Who would be first?

The old grey headed gate guard waved as Page turned onto the red brick entrance to Chamberlain Crossing. "Who's your friend Doll?" "Oh, Lawrence, this is Chenelle Henderson, Marshall High's Homecoming Queen 1994-1995." "Nice to meet you Miss Henderson, I hope you enjoy your visit." "Thank you sir. Page and I are sharing a project for school so I'll see you a few times this weekend." "You can call me Lawrence. It's okay." "No sir, you deserve the same respect I give my father. It's not an old thing. Just respect for your age, you know, like an elder." "Thank you Doll, but I'm used to

Lawrence." "Okay," Chenelle agreed, then as a compromise, dubbed him, "Sir Lawrence." He was so tickled he laughed himself to tears. "We need more young people like you Chenelle. Yes we do!"

Sophia was pawing at the door when Page put the key into the lock. As soon as the door opened, Sophia bolted into the hallway, headed toward the elevator. "Sophia, shame on you!," Page commanded before running inside to get Sophia's leash. "What kind of dog is she?," Chenelle asked. "An Afghan hound. My dad gave her to me for my 12th birthday." "She's beautiful." "Sometimes she's a pain in the butt!" "Who you tellin'! My mom has a poodle named Sade. Sometimes she can be worse than four little sisters!" "If that's anything like a stepsister then I know what's you're saying. If I didn't have her, I'd be an only child. I say stepsister but she's really from my dad's first marriage. Believe it or not, she was born Halloween the same year I was born!" Chenelle looked puzzled. "What's her name?" "Courtney. My dad's divorce papers were still wet when he married my mom. She says he spent a weekend with his ex-wife, to 'finalize matters', before he and mom got married. That's why I have 'The Great Pumpkin' for a sister!" "That's a lot of drama," Chenelle said. "It could be worse," Page laughed. "I could have to live with them in California!" "I guess you're right," Chenelle agreed.

After the girls returned from walking Sophia, Page announced she'd ordered Chinese. "While we're waiting we can watch a movie, okay?" "Okay," Chenelle agreed. Nothing could have prepared her for what happened next. "I'm going to get comfortable. There are juices and bottled water in the 'frig. Help yourself." Chenelle helped herself to a bottle of Evian and sunk into the love seat in front of the TV. Sophia trotted over and placed her nose on Chenelle's leg. "I know what you want girl. You and Sade must have come from the same school." Chenelle scratched Sophia's head vigorously before she noticed a brush lying in front of the plant near the kitchen. Page emerged, in all her splendor, while Chenelle continued brushing Sophia's mane. Page's sudden appearance startled Chenelle. "Where are your clothes girlfriend?" "I never wear clothes when I'm by myself," Page boast. "Well you're not alone Page!" "I'm sorry…" "I know you have the right to do what you want in your house Page but I'm not into that kind of party!" "…I didn't mean to offend you. I'm just more comfortable without clothes on. I hope you're not thinking what Mason said is true?!" Page left the living room. When she appeared wearing a romper, she could she Chenelle was still in deep thought.

Aside from the surprise of seeing Page in the buff, Chenelle couldn't help noticing the tattoo above her pudendum. Just on the fringes of her sparse yet neatly coiffured pubic area, a frantic Tinkerbell struggled to keep an eight ball from reaching Page's labial cleft. "Maybe it is all the confusion from what Mason said at the Halloween party that has me trippin'. Page, I didn't know who Sappho was until Kadeem explained it to me. Then you come out her in your birthday suit and a sista couldn't help but think Mason was right about those Sapphic intentions." "Bianca always tells me my tongue is quicker than my brain. I was just tryin' to emphasize how much I despised Mason when I said that!" The two girls sat nervously pondering if their project was over before it even got started. Chenelle rationalized Page's confidence was natural because she was essentially an only child. She, on the other hand, had grown up with brothers and a father so modesty was second nature. Not since P.E. in the tenth grade had she seen another girl's body. Even then, except for the few minutes she was in the shower, everyone wore a towel draped around themselves. One final memory helped to erase her doubt about Page's persuasion. She remembered the things Damon began saying about her after she refused his advances in the sixth grade. It was time to break the silence.

"Momma calls this growing pains," Chenelle sighed. "What's that?," Page asked eagerly, glad the silence was broken. "Sorting through the confusion caused by rumors and people's immaturity." "Yeah, Bianca says things like that too. She says it's naïve to think, even in the 90's, things between men and women has changed that much. It's the nature of the beast." "Does your moms know you call her Bianca?" "Yeah. It's her idea. She doesn't want to get old. Ever since she and Dad divorced, she's only dated younger men. She says it's payback for the time she lost being married to an older man."

Page knew her mother was home when Sophia started toward the door. It was a game – trying to reach the door before the keys stopped jingling. She lost. "Hi Sweetie, I bought Chinese." "I ordered some before I left school," Page sighed. "Gotcha. I met the delivery boy in the parking lot," Bianca laughed. After dinner Bianca sat and talked with the girls about her day at the office. Page blushed at how candidly she spoke about the twenty-fivish pony-tailed dream boat she'd met. "I'm going to meet that stud muffin at Pan's Lyre and let my inhibitions run wild. You girls enjoy your evening. I'll be home by sunrise!" "See you tomorrow, Bianca," Page said as she kissed her mother's cheeks. "Don't tell too many of your secrets Chenelle. Page loves juicy gossip," Bianca teased. "Just kidding. Behave girls!" Then she was gone. "Your moms is a trip girl! My moms would never pour her tea like that even if she weren't happily married to my daddy!" "Let's forget about Bianca. I want to talk about Damon and Mason. You go first."

Chenelle convinced Page to wait until they'd cleaned up and got ready for bed before they started dredging up more of the past. Finally, Chenelle began the saga of when Damon was her puppy love. "Me and Damon go back to the second grade…," Page marveled over the Tom Thumb wedding and the club house. There was so much fun history between them that Page could understand Damon's obsession with Chenelle. She was just getting ready to tell Chenelle how much she envied her when the walls came tearing down

– the revelation as to why things soured between them "… sixth grade was when it all began to fall apart. My body was starting to change. My first training bra. Cookie and 'Roni's boobs were a little bigger than mine but Pooh and 'Tonya could still get away with wearing t-shirts and slips." "I know the feeling," Page confided, pointing at her modest endowment. "Anyway, Damon went to New York to spend Easter with his cousins. The day he came back he told me, 'I have a present for you but you have to meet me by the school cafeteria at 4' O' clock." "Okay, I know it's something pretty." "Yep, just like Gamma says, 'Sugar and spice and everything nice.' I remember that day so clearly Page, it's scary!" "You don't have to tell all of it Chenelle." "No pressure, I want to. I've only told one other person and you don't have to guess, do you?" "No, it could only be Andrea." "Kadeem would go fool if he knew," Chenelle sighed. "Why, it was the sixth grade!" "I know, but Damon keeps fronting him about what he did with me!" "Okay then, finish," Page encouraged.

"I was wearing this blue paisley sun dress, with a pair of clear red jellies. Damon was standing in the hallway between the cafeteria and the library with a box behind his back. 'Okay, let me see the present,' I told him. 'First I want to show you this game my cousins' play called 'Hide and go get it.'" Page could sense Chenelle's embarrassment when she said, "I didn't have a clue what his plans were. Even after he explained that he girls hide and the boys come and get it!. Damon changed the rules so that he could hide. I agreed to play, to try and find Damon and the box. 'You gotta count to twenty-five and then come find me,' Damon laughed. When I found him he was behind this tall bush on the other side of the library. He gave me the box, grinning from ear to ear."

The anticipation was getting to Page. "So what was in the box," she demanded. "A beautiful lavender Easter Bunny! I was so happy I kissed him. Then he put his tongue in my mouth. I pushed him because I didn't know what else to do." "That's how they kiss in New York Chenelle." "Well it's nasty." "Okay, kiss me again and I won't put my tongue in your mouth." "You better not," I said but I really was curious to know what it was like if you expected it so I did it to him. Everything was okay until I felt his hand in my panties. Then his finger was inside me. It was too quick. We had seen the facts of life film the week before. Amina had already got her first period. I was confused, scared and knew I was too young to be doing anything like that. I asked Damon, 'what are you doing?'" "Well, you said we could play hide and go get it!" He pulled down his pants. Girl, you could imagine the state he was in. All I could remember was Levar telling me what to do when a boy won't leave you alone. I kicked him and ran home!"

"What happened to the bunny," Page laughed. "I'll tell you after you tell me about that tattoo and why you hate Mason Cole so much." "Deal."

"Since my parents are divorced, I have a bi-coastal life-style. My summers are spent in California, the rest of the year, here with my mom. Occasionally she'll let me spend a holiday with him. I think the holiday trip is more out of spite than to allow him to spend some quality time with me during festive periods. Anyway, two years ago, between our sophomore and junior year, I got the tattoo after Courtney and her cronies dared me to. They all got Warner Bros. characters over their bra line or above their ankle. I HAD to go them one better!" "But, why Tinkerbell and the eight ball?" "Well, me being Little Miss Cynical, accepting the fact I will eventually loose my virginity, decided to do something original. Like pool, the game is won when the eight ball goes into the 'pocket' – so is loosing your virtue. Like Tinkerbell had the thing for Peter Pan, the man that I surrender to will be special. So until that time, I'll fight hard to keep my innocence." "I thought you were crazy," Chenelle chimed. "I was sore too. I wore sun dresses every day for a week. The week before I came home, we were at a beach party hosted by Courtney's friend, Dana's brother. He invited some of his fraternity brothers to the party. Later that night everybody paired off walking down the beach, kicking water and just being crazy. Then couples started breaking off into the dunes. The goon I was with just starts going animal on me. He didn't rape me or anything but what he did was just as humiliating." "Look Page, that is your name isn't it?," he joked. "I know 'no means no.' I'm not ready to loose my football scholarship.

If you're not going to go all the way, at least let me give you a pearl necklace to remember our night together!" "What's a pearl necklace got to do with this?," Chenelle asked. "It's disgusting. When I asked him that same question, he yelled across the dunes telling everybody how much of a geek and tease I was." "Well, what is it?" "The thing that hurt the most is Courtney was one of the people who held me down."

Chenelle looked into Page's eyes. Seeing the same pain she saw at the Halloween dance, she reached out supportively. Page continued. "He said it was easier to show me than to tell me. Courtney told me to lay down between her and Dana. As soon as that monster pulled down his swim trunks, Courtney and Dana grabbed my arms. Then Dana's brother grabbed my feet and held them together. I was helpless. While I lay on my back in the moonlit sand, instead of romance, he violated me by spilling his seed across my neck and breast." "You're better than me girl. Courtney, Dana and whoever else would be dead about now!" "It wasn't worth the trouble to try and explain to Dad. Anyway, it washed off." "And I thought Damon took me through!," Chenelle sighed.

Chenelle saying Damon's name brought Page back to the present – Mason. "Mason and I had American History together last year. We stared dating during baseball season. When spring training started for football, I didn't miss a day watching him practice. I thought he was Peter Pan." "Did you go all the way?" "No, I knew I wasn't ready for sex, I just thought he was Peter Pan. Happy go lucky. Free spirited. Patient. For a while he was content to do some heavy petting when we went to the movies but just before school started this year, he changed. I was waiting outside the locker room after the late session of the two-a-days when he and Damon walked out." "I know Damon said something foolish." "He said, 'if you're going to be Spawn's girl, you're going to have to up the booty!' I looked at Mason. All he did was raise his shoulders and say, 'or at least let me give you a pearl necklace.' Before I knew it, I slapped him. All I could see was the beach. He wasn't Peter Pan!' "I feel you Girlfriend. Demonseed and Spawn indeed!"

Back at school. Damon didn't team up with anyone for the project but was just a little irritated when he learned Mason had partnered with Kadeem. Every time he'd invited Mason to hang with him, "run some honies," Mason declined, opting to visit with Chyna. Other times he'd be at the library or on a double date with Kadeem and Chenelle. Feeling he'd suffered the ultimate disrespect, losing a friend to a lame, he decided to confront Mason. "Yo Spawn, you think I'm gonna let you dis' me?" "What are you talkin' about dude?" "Oh, so you wanna play me now?" "I don't follow you Damon!" When Chyna sidled along side Mason, Damon couldn't pass up the opportunity to strike hard. "It's like that now. You'd rather kick it with a punk and a dyke than to hang with a playa. I bet you can 'follow' that dude!"

"She not a dyke," Mason exclaimed. Chyna noticed his hand turning into a fist. She also noticed Mr. Simone exiting the boys' restroom. She cupped Mason's fist in her hands but not before Mr. Simone noticed then tension in Mason's face. Wisdom prevailed. "Chyna, say goodbye to your boyfriend and come into class." Then he warned Damon. "Edwards, football season is over. Do believe me when I say, unofficially of course, I wouldn't loose any sleep over you missing a few days because of a suspension. Bedsides, your friend is a little bigger and tougher than Heike. Get to class." Mason relaxed his fist. He squeezed Chyna's hand while scowling at Damon. "We're not through dude." "Then I guess it's on!" "Save it gentlemen and get to class like I said. Neither of you need a suspension! Chyna blew Mason a kiss. "By the way Damon, jealousy will get you nowhere!" She turned before Damon could respond. Demonseed without Spawn - what a concept.

BITTERSWEET VICTORIES

Track season was scheduled to begin Monday, the 13th, the day before Valentines' Day. 'Roni could hardly contain her excitement. She called the girls and reminded them of their promise to try out for the team. "Let's start running together on the 1st so we'll be ready when Coach Ashford times us on the first day of practice." She forgot Cookie wasn't talking to Chenelle until 'Tonya reminded her. "Girl, you know I'm ready. This broken thumb messed up my basketball season. You know Cookie said she's not going to do anything with Chenelle for two weeks. She's trippin' real hard girl." "I know 'Tonya. I'm tired of her sweatin' that Chelsea thing. She needs to let it go." "Chenelle needs to stop saying Cookie will get over it and make the sister talk to her." "You're right," 'Tonya agreed, remembering the advice her father had given her a few weeks ago. "So, which one of us is going to talk to Cookie and which one of us is going to talk to Chenelle?" "Cookie has forgiven you, but if you start saying she's wrong for not talking to Chenelle, she'll go stupid." "I know that's right. If she'd gone off on me like I did her, I'd want some get back too. You get Cookie and I'll get Chenelle." It was Sunday, the 5th of February, before 'Roni convinced Cookie to forgive Chenelle. They agreed to meet at Davenport Bridge after church. After Page went home, The Summit, The meeting place where all major decisions were made.

'Roni called Pooh to let her know about the meeting. At first 'Roni didn't understand why Pooh was so tentative in agreeing to show up. Red was in the background saying, "Pooh, are you coming with me?" "What's up Pooh? Why is your moms going so crazy?" "My father gets out of prison tomorrow." "So why are you having a hard time deciding if you want to go?" "The last time he was supposed to come home he got into a fight and got another two years added onto his sentence. I don't know if I can take him telling us he's not coming home again." "I'm not going to tell you what to do, but if I couldn't take a walk with my daddy for ten years…" "Exactly. Ten years is so long ago. I barely know what to say to him in my letters. He went away just when I was getting to know him well. Truck drivers are always on the road." "Pooh, are you coming baby?," Red asked again. "If you're not, I'll understand. I just hope you daddy does." "I'm coming Momma. I can't let you make that drive all by yourself. Besides, I know Daddy is looking forward to seeing us in the morning." Back to 'Roni. "I'm sorry I left you hanging. I'm going to go with Momma." "Nobody is going to be mad at you. I'll tell the gang the good news." "Thanks 'Roni. I'll see you Tuesday."

Knowing Cookie wouldn't be able to get the Maxima, 'Roni offered to drive. "That's alright 'Roni, I'll walk. I need to think about what I'm going to say to Chenelle." "Let's both walk then. It's only a couple of blocks to the bridge anyway." "Okay," Cookie agreed. "What did you think about the solo Sis. Rivers sang?" "Master Can You Use Someone?" "Yea girl. She sang that thing, didn't she?!" Cookie stopped talking; lost in thought while the lyrics raced through her mind. Thoughts of how much impact she'd made on Chyna by advising her read Romans; hopes that Chenelle had forgiven her for calling her a "sell out." After all, it was her own frustration that got her in trouble with the dean. The thought weighing heaviest on her mind however, was how she should deal with the inner turmoil Chyna's insinuations provoked.

The air was tentative as 'Roni and Cookie approached the miniature park near the bridge. They were oblivious to Chenelle and 'Tonya's laughter until they noticed its cause. In the distance, Sade stood at the foot of a tree while the squirrel she had been chasing scurried across the telephone lines to the other side of the street. They too joined in the laughter; Laughter that segued into a chorus of apologies, tears and a long overdue group hug. "Reunited," Cookie thought to herself – 'A small circle of friends.' Then she noticed Gina was missing. "Where's Pooh?" "Oh yeah," 'Tonya exclaimed. "Her father gets released from prison tomorrow. She and Ms. Red are driving down to meet him." "Does anybody know what he was in for?," Chenelle asked. "Vehicular homicide." "How did you find out?" "Ms. Red told my mother it was an accident." "So why did he get sent to prison?," Cookie asked "I think it was because he had drugs in his system." "Stop it girl!" "Yeah; that's it. He had already driven more hours than the law allows but he was trying to make some extra money to buy Ms. Red a fox fur for her birthday. Supposedly, he stopped at his usual truck stop, had a cup of coffee and took a Vivarin. Before he left, he bummed a cigarette from another truck driver. Unfortunately, it was laced with PCP." "What happened next," 'Roni asked. "Ms Red started crying. She knew he took Vivarin. She refused to believe he was using. The next thing he remembered, he was being handcuffed by state troopers. Witnesses said he rear ended a charter bus, twice, forcing it into a metal barrier at the beginning of the off ramp. Two people were thrown through the front windshield and the driver was paralyzed from the waist down." "That's awful. No wonder Pooh never talks about her daddy!" "You know, I wouldn't know how to act if my daddy had done something like that."

This knowledge of the Hall's family tragedy far overshadowed the initial reason for the girls meeting. They'd made a pact to be a team again. Every pact between them since the second grade had been kept. Now wasn't the time to break the trend. But it was time to focus on Pooh and Ms. Red; Time to pray for a smooth, happy reunion. Chenelle looked over at the trees. "Come on Sade. Momma's waiting for us."

The week that followed brought with it the anticipation of Valentines Day, the dance and the first symptoms of spring fever. Although Shayla had long since confronted Chereth concerning the disrespect she'd shown her, Chereth continued to gloat over taking Damon from her. The fight everyone wanted to see between Chelsea and Chenelle would take place between these two. Instead of the bathroom, it happened on the lawn near the band room. "Look Cherry, I wouldn't listen to Chenelle when she tried to warn me about Damon. I learned from my mistake." "What are you trying to say?" "I'm not trying to say anything. I AM saying, I'm not going to fight you over a dog like Damon!" In Chereth's mind, Shayla was just suffering from a case of sour grapes. "Aw, you're just mad because your daddy made you have an abortion." "No sista. What I'm mad about is my 'friend' can't see how she's being played like I was. Thank God, I wasn't pregnant. That was a blessing, even if you don't believe me." "I'm being played by who?," Chereth demanded. "You don't know? You better ask somebody!"

By now the rest of the freshmen/sophomore band class began forming a circle around the two teenagers. Some began chanting, "Set it off." "Yeah, we want to see a beat down!"

Shayla tried to walk away. Tangela begged Kenny to stop what was about to happen. "I don't think so; Cherry needs to pay for how she dissed her own home girl!" "You know you're wrong Kenny. Cherry," she pleaded, "You don't want this!" Cherry was feeding off the bloodlust of the gallery. She grabbed Shayla by the arm. Shayla jerked away. "I said I'm not going to fight you!" Cherry wouldn't have it. She slapped Shayla's elbow causing her to loose control of her books and instrument case. When Shayla saw her flute spring from its case, striking the pavement, she lashed out. The crowd was satisfied. They had something to talk about during lunch. "It was over before it started." "Shayla hit her like Mike Tyson." "A three second knock-out." It should have been Damon.

The first day of Track practice was basically an introduction of the coaches and outline of their expectations. Those athletes returning from last year were familiar with Coach Etienne Ashford's story of how she was the white stepsister of the great Evelyn Ashford. They didn't listen as attentively as the newcomers did when she gave her spiel about being the best while having fun. It wasn't until she introduced her new assistant coach that their point of interest changed. "Good afternoon ladies. My name is Raimont Forney. I'm a graduate student at Morgan State. While I'm with you, I'll be gathering material for my thesis on Kinesiology. I'm from a long line of sprinters so you can expect me to be a taskmaster." He paused, looking over his captive audience. "Ladies, my motto is this: Pain is good, feel the burn. Tomorrow is

Valentines Day so I'll take it easy on you. Wednesday and Thursday however, will be dedicated to preparing you for time trials on Friday. They're all yours, Coach Ashford." "Bye Coach Forney," rang the chorus of Lady Panthers. "I have just one question Coach," Keisha Money joked. "What's that?" "Is he married?" "Put your hormones in a sock Missy. You've got enough to worry about with that 800 meter time." "Ooh, you know you're wrong for that Coach." "Okay. Everyone get in some stretching and jog a half-mile. Unlike Coach Forney, I plan to introduce you to some of the joy and pain that leads to victory."

As usual, Cookie came up with a scheme to get the answers concerning Mr. Forney's vital statistics. We'll get Pooh to talk the faculty advisor into letting her interview him for the school paper!" "You go girl. I knew we could count on you to come up with a plan," 'Roni said. Pooh gladly accepted her mission. The interview was equivalent to Pulitzer quality. The picture she took of him demonstrating the proper technique for coming out of the blocks became the embodiment of their collective infatuation. Oprah couldn't have done it better. Oh, but they would learn to hate his workouts.

VALENTINES DAY

With the exception of weekends, it's very rare for the Edwards to have breakfast together. This morning however, Linford made it Priority One for everyone to be home. He was no slouch in the kitchen. His style was a combination of the southern and eastern shore styles his parents used when he was coming up. He carefully de-boned the rainbow trout he served his mother. A side dish of yellow grits and two slices of home made honey basted coconut bread rounded out the spread. Gamma wouldn't let him pour her tea. She liked to sip her tea, hot, so she poured when she desired to. Sharon sat down to two eggs, sunny side up, surrounded by freshly cut strawberries, and two halves of wheat toast covered with a thin layer of strawberry Smuckers. A fresh cup of almond amaretto cappuccino complimented her fare. Last, but not least, Damon. Linford ground two sticks of cinnamon, mixed the powder into the Aunt Jemima batter and poured fifteen silver dollar pancakes. Next, he cut ten slices of Oscar Mayer bacon into thirds. Damon loves curly bacon. The pancakes were arranged in five tiers; the bottom, a ring of five, then four, three, and on until one lone pancake rested atop the mound - The coup de gras – a scoop of butter with blueberry syrup cascading down the slope. "You know Pops, you're alright when you want to be." "A man has to keep his family happy son."

Breakfast over, Sharon kissed Linford at the garage door. "I love you Mister. I'll show it better tonight." Linford laughed when he thought how surprised she'd be when she received the bouquet of Sonia's (peach colored roses) at the bank later on. Gamma told him to leave the dishes for her. She'd do them before Alfre came to take her shopping. It's okay Momma. My first patient isn't scheduled until 10 O'clock." "Don't make me get that ear," she teased. "You've fussed over me enough this morning. I miss your father enough as it is. Always doting over me." "Yes Momma. Come on Damon. You need to be rolling out too." As Damon left the house, Linford handed him an envelope. "Give this to Miss Bennett please." "Olivia?" "Miss Bennett when she's on the J.O.B. Brother. Like you young people say, give her her props." "See ya. I'm out." "Have a good day knucklehead." Linford returned to the breakfast nook to help Gamma. "Clack!" The lightening quick strike of the sugar spoon reminded him when his mother was intent on something, it was so! "I told you boy, I'll do these dishes while I'm waiting for your knee sister." "Careful with that spoon, Momma. These skilled hands are very delicate," Linford joked. "Alright then, come here so I can twist that ear ole' hammer knocker." Much to his dislike, Gamma ran water into the sink and began washing the dishes by hand. "Humble beginnings…," she always said. "…lest we forget." He knew not to protest. Kissing her on the forehead, he said, "I love you Momma."

Gamma didn't hear Damon when he came home. She was asleep. All that walking through the mall got her pressure up so she asked Alfre to bring her home. She did, however, wake up to the tell-tale sounds of pleasure coming from his bedroom. She would spare them both the embarrassment of his indiscretion. She sang, "Ladybug, ladybug, fly away home," as she walked down the hall. The next thing she heard was the shower. She watched from her window as Damon drove away.

Out of respect, Linford and Sharon never entered Damon's room without an invitation; Rite of Passage at age fourteen. However, when Sharon couldn't find the match to her sapphire earrings, she knew Damon had to have it. She sensed a piquant aroma wafting from behind the dresser – definitely not socks. She would confront Damon later. Tonight was her turn to surprise Linford.

FOOLS RUSH IN...
A MOTHERS' DILEMMA

Many times a deal struck in the name of malice, however innocent, gives birth to consequences those striking the deal never anticipated. In celebration of the embarrassment Damon served Chenelle, Chelsea promised Damon a reward only she could give. "I'm babysitting this Saturday in Buchanan Forest. The Swingers won't be back until Sunday afternoon so you come over at 9:30 pm. Cameron Jr. should be asleep by then." "Bet that," Damon agreed.

Damon woke up early Saturday morning. His first order of business was to take Judas out by the horse trail so he could get his exercise, chasing rabbits. After he came home, he bathed Judas, showered and went downstairs to enjoy a bowl of Honey Nut Cheerios. Sharon met him there. Over the last four days she'd given much thought to how she'd approach her child about the mannish things he was doing.

Sure he was about to become a legal adult but he was still living under the roof that she and Linford provided for him. Why couldn't he at least wait until he was off at college to sow his oats? She laughed aloud remembering the system she and her roommate devised to alert one another that they were "entertaining" a guest when she was stationed in Japan. Actually, she and Linford came up with it. Whenever one of them had a guest, they'd place a pieced of typing paper under the door, just far enough for the corner to be seen. The other would get the hint and either fall asleep in the TV lounge or sleep in a friends' room. She was Linford's Disbursing Clerk (pay accountant). He was a Dental Technician assigned to prosthetics. She needed a crown for one of her molars. A mutual interest was sparked and so began the relationship between Sharon Tifton and Linford Edwards.

Anyway, she poured herself a cup of cappuccino and sat across from Damon. "Hey Momma, how you living?," Damon said. "I'm fine, my son, and you?" She casually placed her surprise on the table. Damon needed to buy time. "What are you doing Momma? If I put my underwear on the table you'd go nut!" "Don't play with me Damon. Who's are they?" "Gamma told you, huh? She should mind her own business!" "Your grandmother knows nothing of this conversation. I found them when I was looking for my earring. Were you wearing a condom?" "Why are you in my business? What about my respect as a man?" Damon pushed his plate over the panties and stormed away from the table. "Respect, Damon?

A true man wouldn't resort to childish pranks like bringing someone's underwear to a Christmas party. Did you even think to apologize to Shayla?" "Apologize to Shayla for what? She pushed up on me." "But you didn't have to lay down with her Damon!" Damon looked at his mother in disbelief. Then he committed the ultimate disrespect – he waved her off. "I ain't tryin' to hear this Momma." He started out the garage door. "Have you lost your mind boy?!, Sit down. I don't know what you 'ain't tryin' to hear but you will hear this!" "A man has to handle his business Momma. Only a punk would walk away from a woman trying to give up the guts." Again he turned to leave the house. "Damon, don't walk away from me. I'm not one of those little girls that have you convinced of your manhood. The difference between a man and a boy, my son, is a man has the wisdom to prevent mistakes. When he makes one, he takes responsibility for it!" Damon couldn't bear to hear anymore. Truth hurts. One more faux pas. He had to have the last word. "A woman knows when to stay out of a man's business." In an instant, Sharon grabbed a steak knife, hurling it in Damon's direction. It stuck in the door facing as Damon slithered into the garage. Sharon lapsed into her South Carolina tongue. "Gitout boye. Doon't cum bach onteel you fadda bring you hohm.!" Parental angst. Maternal remorse.

Sharon was so tense when she laid down beside Linford the bed seemed to chill. The strings of the maternal bond were stretching to their limit. Although she didn't give him the proverbial "cold shoulder," when he kissed the back of her neck, he knew her mind was elsewhere. "It's Damon isn't it Mon Cherie?" As much as she wanted to tell him, she still felt compelled to protect her monster. "No Sweetheart, it's just a couple of accounts we had to freeze at the bank." Linford knew different. Gamma had been acting strange since Valentine's Day also. Now, at the beginning of what he'd planned to be a great weekend of family togetherness, Sharon was being just a little more than obliging. Sooner or later, it would all come to light. When he stepped out of the shower, Sharon greeted him with a warmer kiss, helped him dry off and offered to make his breakfast – French toast, two eggs fried hard and a cup of hot orange pekoe tea. "What's wrong, Sharon? What is Damon up to now?" "He's just growing up so fast Linford." "Yes, Love, he'll be eighteen soon. June isn't far away either, but that's not what this is about, is it?" Sharon never answered the question. "Judas needs some more dry food. I don't know if Damon remembered to put that on his list when he left a little while ago. Will you get some when you go out dear?" Damon now had an alibi for missing the quality family time Linford had planned. Sharon also had more time to forgive Damon's mannishness.

Linford spent the whole day trying to bring happiness to the two special women in his life. Nevertheless, his efforts were futile. Judas even appeared to be out of sorts, never straying from beneath the picnic table where Gamma sat. It was as though he remembered he was taken away the last time he was at Mason Park, forcing him to endure ten days of quarantine amongst other mere animals. Linford dropped the ladies and the dog off at the house at about 6 0'clock pm. "Micah invited me over to play cards with the boys. It's been a while since I've hung out with the Old Heads. I hope they don't think I've gotten bourgeois on them." "No Dear. Nona told me they (Old Heads) haven't played cards together for a long time. It seems as if everybody's been caught up in their own business. Go on and enjoy yourself." She knew the card game would eventually turn to the subject of "Damon the Demonseed." It was due time.

Damon spent most of the day kickin' it in East Crenshaw. His aunt, Alfre', treated him more like a baby brother than a nephew so he figured her apartment was as best a place as any to go until he went out to Buchanan Forest to hook up with Chelsea. He ran a couple games of basketball with Alfre's boyfriend, Jawan, ate a whole package of BALL PARK FRANKS, then, laid around the rest of the afternoon watching videos. "Yo, Alfre', the brother needs to take a shower before I break out to hook-up with this honey later on. It's just something about this precious East Crenshaw water!" "What's wrong with the Killian Forest water?" "On the real tip?, Your sister-in-law put me out this morning." "And you didn't do anything to deserve it either, right?" "You're right. The brother didn't do na'than." "Yea, and I'm Boo Boo the Fool. I told you you were getting too mannish." "Now you're getting like them." "Them?," Alfre' asked.

"Momma and Gamma! Look, are you going to let me take the shower or not?" "Go ahead boy. If Linford calls me, my name is Bennett...!" "Like I need you to watch my back." "See, you don't know when you got it good, always burning bridges." Damon took his shower, made one last attack on the refrigerator and said, "I'm out." Alfre' just waved. "Jawan, I got the two bottles of Alize. Thanks." He could hear Alfre' yelling at Jawan for buying alcohol for a minor, no matter who that minor was. On to the roulette wheel.

Buchanan Forest was just a wee bit less affluent than Killian Forest. The more expensive homes ranged in the $240-$250 range. Chelsea was babysitting for Cameron Swinger, the pariah of his distinguished military family - A lineage of high ranking officers tracing back to the Mayflower and beyond; the most renowned being his great-great-great grandfather, a Confederate General and landowner. Cameron however, shunned his acceptance to the Citadel. He chose to attain prominence on the classical music circuit. Notwithstanding, "Old Money" spends well.

Damon arrived early, about an hour before Cameron junior's bedtime.. A very rambunctious six year-old to say the least. He nearly ran Damon ragged before he finally tired; demanding Damon put him to bed. Chelsea waited in the kitchen while Damon continued his charade as the dutiful vassal to young Sire Cameron. She sipped casually from the champagne glass filled with the Alize Damon brought. She would enjoy keeping this promise. Damon wasn't Jarad Henderson but he was a hunk. She'd listened to his braggadocio for two years. She heard tales. She wanted to write a page too. "Fools rush in…!" Damon marveled at the glassy luster of Chelsea's lilac colored eyes as she stood before him. "I poured you a glass too," she giggled, leading him into the den. He sat; entranced by the dancing flames reflecting off the pearlescent spheres Chelsea would soon reveal to be contacts, much to his chagrin. It was not long before Bacchus reared his lascivious head. Nature. Curiosity. Impulsiveness. Gratification. The four elements of Hedonism danced around them, satyr and nymph, leading them on a libidinous journey to oblivion. Oblivious to place, unconcerned about time, the pair embarked upon a passionate pilgrimage that rivaled the revelry of Mardi Gras.

They forgot about Cameron. His parents never went to bed until they were sure he'd been asleep for at least two hours. They were not prudes, just prudent. Cameron awoke to the most primal moans imaginable to a six year-old. "Why are those noises coming from Mommy and Daddy's room?," he asked himself. What he saw when he peeped through the doors, slightly ajar, scared him to death. He ran down stairs and dialed 911. "Operator, this is Cameron." The neighbors were a little nervous about the purple Tracker parked on the pool side of the driveway. When the 911 call came in, within an hour after an anonymous call, the hysterical kid warranted attention. "What's your name little one?" "Cameron…" "Stay on the phone Cameron, we're sending someone out now, okay?" "Okay, but hurry up. He's hurting Chelsea." "Who's hurting Chelsea?" "Damon. He's a football player." The operator correctly concluded this incident wasn't anything more than a high school tryst, but dispatched a unit anyway. Better to err on the side of caution. Upon receiving the transmission that a unit was on the scene, the operator directed, "Go open the front door Cameron and let the police officer in." "Okay."

Chelsea and Damon were surprised by the knock on the bedroom door. "Boy, Cameron has a heavy hand," Damon said. "Open the door Mam, it's the police." The pair scrambled to put their clothes on before Chelsea went to the door. After taking a visual assessment of the room, the office directed Chelsea to put Cameron back to bed and come downstairs so he could talk with her and Damon. He'd come to the same conclusion as the operator. All would have gone away without a hitch had Damon just kept his mouth shut. Instead, he launched into a tirade, accusing the office of racism, harassment and lack of appreciation for beautiful women. He continued to insult the officer, even after being informed of the possibility of his being charged with trespassing (he wasn't invited into the Swinger home by the owners) and a few other charges. Finally, it was Damon's laughter and posturing that led to his arrest for being drunk and disorderly. Two additional charges, transporting alcohol and giving alcohol to a minor, were added after the officer's partner found the empty Alize bottle in the den and the bottle in Damon's Tracker.

Sharon and Gamma sat in the den watching a special on the rise in teenage crime. Judas, as usual, lay at Gamma's feet. When a depiction of gang shooting flashed onto the screen, Judas sat up and began barking at the picture. The phone was ringing. "Shhh, Judas!" "I'll get it, Gamma," Sharon said. "Mrs. Edwards, they're taking Damon downtown," the unfamiliar voice said. "Who is this?" "Oh, I'm Chelsea McDavid." Sharon remembered she was the head cheerleader. Circumstantial evidence. The puzzle was taking shape. "Thank you, Chelsea!," Sharon said diplomatically. Then she called Linford. "Go get you son, Linford. He's in jail." "I asked you before I left home what was going on with Damon. Are you ready to tell me now? The fellas' have been throwing hints at me all night and now you call me and tell me he's in jail. What's going on Sharon?" "Just go get him please. We'll talk about it when you get here." "Leave him there until tomorrow. Maybe he'll think about whatever it is he's gotten himself into!" "Never mind, Edwards, I'll go get him!" Sharon argued with herself all the way to the precinct. "You know you should have told Linford when Shayla went for her surgery!" She should definitely have told him about this morning.

THE MASSACRE...
REVELATION

Linford excused himself from the game about one hour after Sharon called. The time had come for the confrontation he'd dreaded since Damon began Junior High School. The Old Heads knew the nature of the phone call and Linford's subsequent withdrawal from the game even without him saying so. As he cashed in his chips, each looked at him as if to say, "We told you so." Linford acknowledged their unspoken advice with a nod. "Keep a cool head," Micah said, squeezing Linford's shoulder as he walked out the door – off to Killian Forest.

The kitchen door was open when Linford pulled into the garage. He didn't hear Sharon asking Damon was Chelsea the hussy he'd brought into her/their house. He did, however, hear Damon's denial before telling Sharon a woman had no right questioning a man about his "business." He saw him stop Sharon's intended slap in mid-swing. The straw that broke the camel's back – Damon pointed at his mother and demanded respect. "It is you boy, who owes me respect, and thanks! You don't know how many times I've kept your father from beating your butt. God bless you when he does get here. I've done all I'm going to do, Damon!" Pride and arrogance refused to remove themselves from Damn's eyes. He refused to acknowledge the axiom, "The bigger they are…" Intuition warned gamma to take Judas outside. Linford was going to make a believer out of Damon.

"The Old Heads tried to tell me you'd gone crazy, my son. Now I believe them. Your mother's been better than good to you. I don't even put my finger in her face and I've been married to her for nineteen years!" "So what are you tryin' to say?," Damon taunted. "All these years, your mother got me to listen to the advice of Dr. Spock. I've tolerated all this New Jack badness, the shaved head, the scarf and the earring. Now I'm going to teach you a few things that in the words of my generations' Spock, you might 'live long and prosper!" "You're going to teach me how to respect women? Better yet, maybe you're going to teach me to respect my momma?" "Your momma second; first and foremost, my wife!"

Damon grinned at his father indignantly. "You done bumped your head old man. All those boxing trophies you have from the Navy don't mean anything here. Six-foot-two, two hundred pounds and change versus five-foot-ten, a buck-ninety maybe. You need to go somewhere and play your saxophone Pops!" "So you think you're ready for me to get in your ass, Mr. Edwards?" "No. It's me who's going to get in yours' for dissin' my mother. I read your note to Olivia. 'Dear Pookie...signed, Little Daddy.' Then I threw it away. How you gonna front like that. All those years you had your b@#$* in our house pretending she was just the babysitter. Who was dissin' Momma then?" "So that's why she didn't show for lunch. You're not as smart as you think, son. That b@#$*, Olivia, is your big sister." "You're a liar," Damon yelled. Then he tried to sucker punch his father; a punch that only hit air.

"You've got to come better than that brother!" Damon's next punch was countered by a right hook to the ribs, loosing a loud gasp. Then a left to the sternum. The straight right to the stomach released warm memories of when Damon was six years old. He fell to his knees as his embarrassment trickled down his leg. Though he didn't want to admit it, he'd had enough. He reluctantly heeded his fathers' direction to apologize to his mother. His embarrassment gave way to the revelation of Olivia's being his sister. "But how," he asked himself while he showered. He decided to ask Olivia, Miss Bennett, on Monday.

Olivia picked up on Damon's ambivalence as he approached the tennis court. She waved him over to the far court, where she was demonstrating the two-handed backhand swing to the tennis team. Over lunch, Linford had told her about the confrontation between him and Damon. She would explain it all to her little brother. It felt good when she "pretended" to be his big sister back in the day. Now it was real. He was happy to know the truth but he felt all the more betrayed. For eighteen years he was told he was his parents' only child. Actually he misunderstood the truth of being called only son to mean only child. "It's no one's fault really, Damon. You have to understand my grandparents' feelings. My mother was only fourteen. OUR FATHER was also. Marriage wasn't an option as far as my grandparents were concerned. They hated Little Daddy. When Momma died in childbirth…" The tears forming in her eyes kept her from finishing the tale of two siblings.

During Pooh's interview, Coach Forney reluctantly told her of his nickname, Geordi LaForge; this for his grey contacts which made him look like the Star Trek character. He was directing his girls to hurry out to the track when Keisha and Cookie stopped short, pointing at the awkward scene on the tennis court. "Look girl. Isn't that Damon hugging Miss Bennett?," Keisha asked. Though Cookie was given to fits of rage, her response was totally unexpected. There isn't enough space on this page to describe what she said about Damon. "What's this all about Cookie? You're acting like Damon is your man!" "You need to mind yours Keisha!" "Bet that, Sister Girl! I'm going to go watch Geordi, watch us. I still don't know why you're trippin' so hard over a buster like Damon." Mr. Forney was trippin' too. His concern however, was why this teacher was openly embracing a student. Olivia promised to tell him after practice. Who would have believed?

TIME TO GET SOMEWHERE

After two and one half weeks of practice the girls were ready for some action. They'd had enough of build-ups, straight-aways, curves, and exercise. Too much practice without vindication, a whole lot of pain, now for the joy. It was the 3rd of March. What they got when they faced East Crenshaw was pure agony.

East Crenshaw hosted this meeting of feline powers. The Tigerettes had gone to the extremes to display their pride. In addition to their orange and black singlet, each member of the Tigerette sprint corps wore shoulder length tiger striped braids. Colors and pride go hand in hand. Initially, the Lady Panthers scoffed at the Tigerettes. In the end however, they would be served a large helping of humble pie. All meet long, from the gun to the finish line, all were pulled into the vortex of the orange and black blur. With the exception of one first place finish, the naturally swifter Panthera Pardus team, were mere also-rans in the wake of Panthera Tigris.

Coach Ashford stood in the front of the bus reviewing the meets' results. "See where being focused will get you ladies? Except for Keisha's first place finish in the 800 meters, we could do no better than a few seconds and thirds." "Money talks and…." Keisha started. "I guess the rest of y'all need to start eating Frosted Flakes." After the laughter subsided and the t-shirts stopped flying in Keisha's direction, Coach Ashford gave Coach Forney center stage. "In the jungle ladies, it's survival of the fittest. Of the two cats represented today, your namesake is the swifter. She also possesses the most endurance. Keisha did her part so she will get the first Nike statuette. The rest of you fell short. Slow out of the blocks. No transition. Sleeping in the turns, and the four by one, Ladies, I'm still shooing away the flies. I will say no more. Monday, it's on!"

Now that the cat was out of the bag, Heike began to visit Mother Graham on a daily basis. It wasn't very long before Mother Graham began bragging about her granddaughter's track and field prowess. It was only fitting for Heike to be a hurdler. In fact, it was the hurdles that brought her son Omar together with her daughter-in-law, Darla. They ran into each other while both were training for a field meet during his first tour of duty in Germany. The rest is history. T.J. was just as proud of his cousin as their grandmother. Since the beginning of school he pleaded with Heike to try our for the Lady Panthers track team. "Come on Bae, you gotta represent the Graham name." She continued to shy away from the opportunity to "represent" the family name until 'Roni approached her one afternoon. "A little bird told me you had skills – a natural born hurdler." T.J. had played his ace in the hold – peer pressure. She too was one of the fold that had fallen prey to the Tigerette frenzy.

Saturday morning the girls held their usual meeting at Davenport Bridge. 'Tonya started the conversation offering her justification for being slow out of the blocks. "I don't know what he expects from me. I just got that stupid cast off so I can't put a lot of pressure on my wrist." "Oh girl, that's a tired excuse," Cookie chimed. "Oh yeah, well I didn't see you clearing those hurdles so clean either Miss Thing!" 'Roni took it upon herself to stop the name calling and the ensuing argument. "We're just rusty. I think we need a gimmick too! We have to give East Crenshaw props. Those sisters looked tight with those tiger striped extensions!" "Black and black equals, BLACK," Cookie teased. "You know what I mean, A-N-D-R-E-A." "Don't go there V-E-R-O-N-I-C-A." "Why don't you, I mean we, all get a panther tattooed over our ankles?," Pooh offered. "Are you crazy?," Chenelle answered. Then she thought about Page. "Talking about tattoos…"

By now everyone had received their extra credit grades. Chenelle held center stage as she told the gang about her visit with Page. When she announced, "The girl has a tattoo of Tinkerbell on her poonie!," they all cringed in pain. "That's disgusting," Cookie exclaimed. Even after Chenelle explained Page's logic for getting the tattoo, Cookie remained on edge. The mere mention of Page brought Chyna to mind and the thought provoking things she'd said. "Come on y'all. I'm ready to go." Pooh, Chenelle, Heike, 'Tonya and 'Roni exchanged a bewildered glance. Cookie looked into the distance. Time would tell why.

There were two weeks between the East Crenshaw debacle and the St. Patrick's Invitational hosted by St. Julius Cardinals. In the interim, the Lady Panthers enjoyed a small taste of revenge hosting a triangular meet against Taft and Douglas. Keisha stayed true to form winning the 800 while finishing third in the mile. Coach Forney put her in the event to familiarize her with the training regimen she would eventually be subjected to in college. Cookie and Heike finished a very close first and second in the hurdles. 'Tonya contributed by winning the high jump and anchoring the 4x400 MR (meter relay).

'Roni was the show stopper, winning the 100M and 200M dashes. She was no less remarkable when, as the third leg of the 4x100MR, she turned a ten meter deficit into a ten meter lead. A solid baton pass to Chenelle sealed the victory. She was serious about a gimmick to bolster the teams' confidence. A thought came to her as she sat under the dryer at Sojourner's. It was triggered by one of Zhane's videos. "That's it. We'll sing 'Listen to the Vibe' before we step onto the track." Of course she had to call a meeting at Davenport Bridge. This time, she invited as many of the team members as were interested. She even invited the fellas. It had been a while since they'd had a picnic in the park. Keisha was immediately fascinated with 'Roni's idea. "As long as I get to say, 'Listen up, listen up, listen up,' I'm down with it." The impromptu meeting was over quickly. The picnic was a hardy release from Coach Forney's rigorous workouts and a mending process from the chaos incited by the extra-credit project – however enlightening it was.

While the girls formulated their fight song, the guys discussed the chasm that had grown between them. Malik was quick to label Kadeem's "Irkle-ish" grand standing as its origin. Malcolm was just as quick to squash the finger pointing. If unchecked, it would only serve to defeat the purpose 'Roni had brought them together. Cooler heads prevailed. High Five's all around. Brothers. Cookie was ready to go. Malik was content with the closeness holding hands implied, outwardly at least. In his heart of hearts, he struggled to find the supportive warmth normally conveyed by this gesture. "What's up Cookie?," he asked. Her only answer was a cursory smile.

TELL-TALE SIGNS

how-time. Friday, the 17th of March. Eighteen schools from throughout the Tri-state area were represented at the St. Patrick's Day Invitational. The preliminary heats in the individual events were held between 10:00 AM and 3:00 PM. Bradford advanced to the finals in every event. The finals would begin at 4:30 PM – allowing time for parents, students and teachers to hurry over to St. Julius to support their respective teams. During the hours and one-half intermission the girls stayed loose sitting in the infield sipping on Gatorade and munching on Fig Newtons. Keisha and 'Roni provided the comedy. The drama would come later.

Kadeem, Malik, Malcolm and Jacques arrived at about 3:45 PM. They walked over to coaches Ashford and Forney, sitting in the stands discussing their strategy for the relays. Once satisfied that each of their girlfriends were representing, they walked onto the infield to talk with their ladies for a hot ten minutes before Coach Forney made them start warming up. Despite the jovial atmosphere surrounding the circle of purple and gold, Malik was still full of anxiety. He found himself in a quandary, trying to figure out why Cookie was keeping her distance – a situation which was only obvious to him. Everyone else was caught up in the collective buzz coming from the sea of colors amassed inside the quarter mile oval. He went into an even deeper funk when Cookie didn't hesitate to trot over to the long jump pit where Damon stood talking to Miss Bennett.

The Tisdales arrived at 4:15 PM. Victoria motioned Cookie over to the stands so she could see her niece, Andrea, her four year old namesake. When Lil' Drea refused to hug her aunt, Victoria's maternal antennae went up. The next distress signal was sounded when Cookie began to tip-toe as she turned to walk back toward the team. "Time to warm-up. Bye, 'Drea." Missionary Tisdale shook her head. You see, for the passed three generations, every woman on her side of the family walked on their tip toes during the first trimester of their pregnancies. Her other daughters hadn't escaped this quirk, why would Cookie. "Oh Lord, say it ain't so. I'm not ready to go through with my child like Pinkie did with Shayla. If it is so Lord, I thank you for a nice boy like Malik." "Are you talking to yourself Grandma," Lil' 'Drea laughed; "You so silly." Out of the mouth of babes.

Keisha sprang into action when the announcer welcomed the fans and participants to the finals section of the St. Julius/

St. Patrick's Invitational. "Listen up, Listen up, Listen up!," Keisha led in. Her teammates began to chant, "Panthers, Panthers, Purple and Gold, we are swift, we are Bold!" Then in unison, they yelled, "YOU GO GIRLS!" Obviously startled by the Marshall cheer, a flock of turtledoves took flight from beneath the score board. The stadium was enveloped in a cloud of Olympic surrealism. The Lady Panthers performed with an equal amount of pomp and precision. 'Roni, 'Tonya, Chenelle and Cookie lined up, four abreast, across lanes #5 – 8. Taking up the rear of the lines, five deep, were four more seniors, Heike and Keisha being the last two. Once lined up, they formed a single line in lane eight. 'Roni lead the team around the track at a light pace. Keisha started passing the baton from the rear. Once it reached 'Roni, she placed the baton on the track for Keisha to start the cycle again. The group fanned out four abreast again for the last 100 meters of the jog. Malcolm and Jacques stood up in the bleachers yelling, "those sistas are the bomb!" Coaches Forney looked at Coach Ashford as if to say, "I hope they can deliver the goods!" They did.

Each relay was poetry in motion. The personification of Zephyr. In the high and long jumps, the Lady Panthers floated like feathers. The Nike statuette went to Cookie for her stunning second place finish in the hurdles. Slow out of the blocks, she struck the first hurdle and barely cleared the next two. Each successive hurdle loomed larger than life but she met the challenge undaunted by the threat of losing. Surprisingly, Lana Mullis of St. Julius was the only person between her and Heike after the last hurdle. East Crenshaw and Taft were reeled in after the fourth hurdle. Pure desire propelled Cookie to the finish line ahead of Lana. "Congratulations," Lana said after hugging Cookie. "You beat me twice today; One inch in the long jump and one step in the hurdles. We'll meet again at state." "See you when you get there, girlfriend," Cookie said sportingly. Heike noticed a scant trickle of blood on Cookie's inner thigh as they walked back to the starting line to pick up their sweats. Assuming the worst, she whispered to her teammate and arch nemesis, "I have an extra light day in my bag if you need it." "I wish that was my problem," Cookie sighed. "I scraped the second hurdle. Thanks anyway." She put on her sweats before walking toward the stands on her tiptoes.

Carmen could barely contain herself when the girls came through the door. She wanted to give 'Roni the letter from Tennessee State at the track meet. It was an invitation to visit the campus which could possibly be her home for the next four to five years. Cookie, Chenelle, and 'Tonya decided it was best to let Carmen and 'Roni share this "Kodak moment" as a family. They would hear all about it later.

Cookie's joy from being the recipient of the coveted Nike statuette was short-lived. Her reception wasn't quite as warm as 'Roni's. "Auntie, Grandma was talking to herself at the races. It was so funny." It wasn't funny to Cookie when her mother sent Lil' 'Drea into the den to play the video game. Missionary Tisdale only talked to herself when she was preparing to have a serious discussion with someone. "Andrea, I haven't talked to your father about my suspicions yet. I want you to go into your room and read I Corinthians, Chapter seven. After you finish, we'll talk." "I already know what that chapter says about virgins and marriage, Momma." "So, what does Malik know about fornication?" "Momma, Malik and I aren't doing anything. Why are you trippin' so hard!?" "Don't bring that slang into my house, Andrea Yvette! I know you've been doing something because you're walking on your tiptoes." Cookie cursed herself under her breath. She had inherited the Baines curse too. "I promise you Momma, Malik and I aren't doing anything." For the next two weeks Cookie made a conscious effort to walk flat footed.

SNOW BALLS...

The harder Cookie tried to mask her indiscretion, the more obvious it became to her mother. Yet every time Missionary Tisdale brought the subject up, Cookie denied anything had happened between her and Malik. Finally, at her wits end, Missionary Tisdale called Nona to forewarn her of the possibility that Chenelle might be fornicating. "You know those two are like two peas in a pod. Cookie's trying to hide it from me, but I've seen the signs. My baby is with child." After she got off the phone with Nona, she called Elaine Hammond. "Your son is going to be the father of my next grandchild," she announced. Elaine took offense to the accusation. "Before you start trying to clean my house, you should make sure there isn't any dirt in yours. There's something going on between Malik and Andrea but it's not what you think. Just last week I heard him and Malcolm talking about how much time she spends talking to Damon now days. When I heard that, I began to understand why he's been moping around the house for the last month." "Excuse me Elaine. I wasn't trying to start an argument. I'm just trying to..." "What you're trying to do is lose a friend over something you think happened. Did you know your daughter refused to accept Malik's Valentine's Day present? In fact, the chocolates are still in my refrigerator." Then Elaine dropped the bomb. "You know Missionary, you've had your head to the sky so long, you've forgotten us mere mortals. Malcolm did mention that Andrea didn't show up for school on Valentines Day. I don't remember you saying anything about her being sick," she added. Suddenly, Missionary Tisdale felt heart sick. She remembered coming home that afternoon to find Cookie already there, in bed. She never questioned the excuse Cookie gave her about pulling a muscle in her back and leg while she and Miss Bennett were showing some moves to the majorette section. Why would she lie about something like that. "I've got to go, Elaine. I'll see you at choir practice, right?" "Lord willing," Elaine answered. She listened for an apology but it never came.

When Malik came home from school, he found his Bible opened to I Corinthians, Chapter 7, with the following verses highlighted:

1) "Now concerning the things whereof ye wrote unto me: It is good for a man not to touch a woman.

2) Nevertheless, to avoid fornication, let every man have his own wife, and let every woman have her own husband."

Now he was totally perplexed. The only person he'd ever given serious thought to being with was barely speaking to him. He searched his mind for what and who caused his parents to leave this unspoken message for him. At dinner that evening, he set the record straight with verse 37 of that very same chapter. He was careful to preface his statement with a declaration of love and respect for his parents. The he began his explanation. " 'Tonya made a joke at the Homecoming dance about 'Roni rewarding Malcolm for scoring three touchdowns. Even though that's all it was, everybody agreed there are too many unwanted babies being born, especially in 'our' community. We all have plans after high school that don't include becoming parents before our time. I don't know which one of you left the message for me but I want to give this back to you. In verse 37, it says:

'"Nevertheless he that standeth steadfast in his heart, having no necessity, but hath power over his own will, and hath so decreed in his heart that he will keep his virgin, doeth well."

"Well said my son," Ronald Hammond laughed. "It wasn't me; it had to be your mother." "Yes, it was me, Sweetheart. I got a phone call from Missionary Tisdale at work today. I didn't think you were doing anything but I came home at lunch and left your Bible open to that passage." "Cookie and I are barely talking. She's been tripping over Chenelle and Damon since the football playoffs." "Well, Malik, we're glad you know where you want to go. A lot of eighteen –year-olds are losing the fight to their hormones," Ronald praised his son. "I'm not the one, Old Man." "Watch yourself, Pal," Ronald joked. Nothing else was said.

Saturday morning Malik called the fellas and asked them if they wanted to go over to East Crenshaw and run a few games of basketball. They agreed to meet at Langford's barber shop. Mr. Langford occasionally allowed sidewalk vendors to display their wares inside the shop. Today would bring trouble with it. Anyway, once the Bradford crew arrived at the barbershop, they proceeded to the court across the street from Crescent Villas. They numbered seven. Malik, Malcolm, Jacques, Foots, T.J., Kadeem and Kenyon. "Why did you bring him?," Malcolm asked Kadeem. "I called Chenelle to tell her to meet me over here at about 2:00 PM and the next thing I know she's asking me to let Kenny run with us." "Ah man, I can't believe you went out like that!" "Like what Malcolm? Pooh is coming too," Foots declared. "Please, my brothers, don't be so sensitive. I'm just warming up for these East Crenshaw boys. You know I gotta talk them out of their game." "Save it for the court then," T.J. chastened.

The snow ball began to take on even more momentum. After the showdown with his father, Damon decided it was better for him to stay with his Aunt Alfre'. Crescent Villas was a modest apartment complex. Unfortunately, a few of the tenants had questionable employment. After a few games, Malcolm walked across the street to get a bottle of Gatorade. It was then that he noticed a familiar jeep. He couldn't help himself. Playing the devil's advocate, he started in on Malik as soon as he returned to the court.

"Yo, Malik, isn't that Damon's Tracker across the street?" "Why are you asking me? I'm not his keeper!" "Since you went there, my brother, I want to know why it seems like he's 'keeping' more time with your lady than you are?" "We're supposed to be boys. Right her, Malcolm," Malik yelled, pointing to his heart. "If you had my back like you say you do, you would be telling me what's wrong instead of asking me. I'm happy for you and 'Roni, my brother. At least she doesn't have your parents doubting you. Let me handle my business without my best friend always trying to throw salt on my wounds." Malik wasn't the only one taken aback by Malcolm's jesting. Kadeem knew all too well what it felt like to have Damon's specter looming over his love life. "Let's go get something to drink," he offered. Malik put his ball cap on, following Kadeem off the court.

"That's foul," Foots said. T.J. threw the basketball into Malcolm's stomach, catching him off-guard. "Let's play some 21 while we're waiting for the next downs." Malcolm had to catch his breath as a result of the hard toss. Kenny was laughing. Malcolm had to get props. "What are you laughing at, punk?!" "You ain't scared of me either, Malcolm," Kenny taunted. The last of the Henderson brothers – he wasn't backing down.

Chenelle, Pooh, and 'Roni arrived at 2:00 PM on the dot. Malik and Kadeem were sitting this game out while Foots and the rest sought redemption for the game they'd lost before the "stupidity" broke out. 'Roni picked up on the tension immediately. So did Chenelle. They looked at Kadeem, who conversely pointed at Malcolm. "He (Malcolm) was dippin', teasing Malik about Damon skeezing with Cookie." "Malcolm, you done bumped your head. Cookie can't stand that fool. Everybody knows that!" " 'Roni is right Malik," Chenelle added. Then she whispered to Kadeem that she needed to talk to Malik. Alone. Kadeem picked up his bottle of Gatorade, put his arms over 'Roni and Poohs' shoulders and strode down to the other side of the court. "I'm the new Mack Daddy!"

Damon. Trouble. Trouble. Damon. He just can't help himself. Demon seed. He left Alfre's apartment enroute to Langford's. He couldn't believe his eyes when he saw the Bradford crew on this side of the bridge. He was especially amused when he saw Malik and Chenelle talking on the bench on the far side of the court. It wasn't his intension to get into a shouting match. He just wanted to say hello. "What's up my peoples? Figured you'd come over and flex for awhile did ya? It looks like these East Crenshaw brothers are scraping you guys up pretty bad – breaking you off some.!"

"But even the worst of us has better game than you, skeezer," Malik shouted. "I got more game in my baby toe than you, buster!" "Sounds like a one-on-one game to me," Jawan yelled from the end of the court. "I wouldn't waste dog sweat on a buster like you, Damon," Malik yelled – then he spit on the ground. The crowd grew silent. Then Damon spoke. "Ask your girl where she was Valentines Day! I have a box for her too," he laughed. It was Kadeem who busted his lip. Jawan stepped between them. "Save it for another day Damon. You're in enough trouble as it is. Weren't you on your way to get a 'cut' when you left the house?"

Langford's Barbershop was under surveillance. East Crenshaw Police Department suspected it was a front for drug and weapons trafficking. The undercover policeman saw Kadeem punch Damon. He watched Damon enter the barbershop and approach the hustler hocking his wares. A variety of "custom made jewelry" was displayed in a briefcase spread across one of the empty chairs. Damon reached into the display, picking out a nickel plated whistle on a silver chain. He marveled at its 3" inch length and fancy finger hole at its base. "How much for this pretty thing here?," he asked. "Seventy dollars." "You done bumped your head if you think I'm going to give you that much money for this!" "My man, I saw how that brother stole you on the basketball court." "And?" "If you put your pinkie in that hole and pull it out, you could keep things like that from happening to you!" Damon did as he was instructed. To his surprise, he was holding a stiletto two inches long and 1/8 inch wide. "Nice, isn't it," the hustler asked. Before Damon could answer, there were two uniformed officers standing in the door, locked and loaded. The undercover policeman walked over to Damon and took the stiletto out of his hand. "I'll take this!" He read Damon the Miranda while walking him out to the second patrol car. The first car took the hustler, who in addition to more custom jewelry, had vials of crack in the false lining of his briefcase. "Don't say anything Damon," Jawan cautioned, "I'm going to get Alfre'. We'll meet you at the police station."

After Kadeem punched Damon, he thought it would be best to get the crew back across the bridge. Especially after he saw E.C.P.D sneaking up on the barber shop. The group made plans to go to the movies later. Jacques declined the offer to tag along since 'Tonya had gone "to the country" to look at another puppy. First things first. Chenelle needed to talk to Cookie. Malik was too hurt and angry to.

Chenelle drove down the block to Banneker Elementary. She had a feeling the issue at hand went beyond the days when they became old enough to hang out at Davenport Bridge. "Andrea, what's up with you, sister?" "Oh, so you been talking to my momma? My name is Cookie to my friends if you remember correctly!" "Your 'friend' wouldn't have had to hear from someone you're supposed to hate that you were with him on Valentines Day instead on going home sick!" "Why are you sweatin' me Chenelle? If you were really my girl, you would understand." "That's why I'm asking you what's up. Did you know your mother called the Hammond's and told them Malik was going to be the father of the baby you're going to have? That was after she called my mother and told her I was probably the person who forged the note from Miss Bennett." Cookie began to cry. She dipped into the Well of Emotion and began pouring out the stagnant waters of Jealousy and Confusion. "I've been jealous of you ever since you got to marry Damon in the Tom Thumb wedding. When you told me about what happened that Easter in the sixth grade, I wished it was me. It's always been about you. Head Cheerleader, Co-Captain at the playoffs and on top of everything else – Homecoming Queen. I've been going crazy!"

By now, Chenelle too, was in tears. She reached to comfort her bestest friend in the world. She held her in a maternal embrace hoping to absorb her pain. Cookie's voice began to quiver. Chenelle couldn't believe what she heard next. "Be careful who you let hug you. You never know who might have Sapphic intentions," Cookie laughed. The friendly embrace they shared suddenly turned nauseatingly cold. "What possessed you say something that sick Cookie?" When Cookie made reference to the extra credit project, Chenelle remembered the awkward situation she was confronted with when Page approached her sans clothing. "Chyna accused me of being secretly in love with you when we were working on our project. I told her my love for you was a sisterly thing but she kept saying I was running from my 'true' feelings. Then she asked me why else would I get so crazy when someone else seemed to be getting too close to you. That's why I skipped class on Valentine's Day to be with Damon. I had to prove her wrong. I convinced myself, since it was Valentine's Day, it was okay." "I can't believe you went out like that Cookie," Chenelle said. Cookies' response added more confusion.

"I thought nobody would ever find out, then, I started walking on my tiptoes." Chenelle frowned. "It's a family curse," Cookie explained. "Every woman on my momma's side, for the last three generations, walked on their tiptoes when they got pregnant." "What are you gonna' do 'Drea?" "It's Cookie, Chenelle – you're going to help me fix it!" "I'm sorry for calling you 'Drea girl, but this is crazy. You never let somebody convince you to do something you didn't want to do; especially somebody like Chyna Nance!" "Okay, so I did it with Damon because he's a Mack Daddy. I don't want to go off to see the world as a virgin. Malik is too 'saved' to do it with me. Is that a better reason for you to believe?" "Don't go there. Sarcasm ain't gonna get it Cookie. You must have really been confused to let yourself make a mistake like that. TLC and Queen Latifah have been singing/preaching about protection forever – 24-7. But you're my girl. WE ARE GOING TO FIX IT!" Ace boon coons.

Monday they took their secret to Miss Bennett, hypothetically, of course. She'd always been there for her girls. A confidante. Never passing judgment. She gave them the number of an old college friend. A soror. It wasn't a question of ethics. Rather one of empathy. Without revealing her secret, she could save another child from becoming the victim of youthful impetuousness. As long as she could remember, her thoughts were of how nice it would have been to know her parents – TRULY know them.

TARNISHED SPOONS

Many a reputation has been sullied by rumor or/ and conjuncture. Such was the case with Malik and Chenelle. After the Christmas fiasco, Missionary Tisdale had no problem joining Mother Graham to remind Nona how "fast" Chenelle was as a little girl. "We don't see why you're so surprised that the truth is out," were the words now vexing Victoria Tisdale's spirit. She would eventually apologize for her presumptions. Accepting the fact that Cookie had actually been with Damon meant she had to face her own haughtiness and prejudice. It was even harder to face Sharon Edwards. Over the past eleven years she'd made sure the other mothers knew how sorry she felt for Sister Edwards - how she praised God Damon wasn't her son.

Missionary Tisdale called Sharon to remind her about choir practice Friday night. "We need to talk afterwards." Sharon informed her that she wasn't planning to come to practice but she wouldn't mind having her over for brunch tomorrow,

Saturday, April First. Missionary didn't want to go to Killian Forest but Sharon wouldn't agree to any other meeting place. Linford would be at the golf course and Damon was still in jail. They could talk in peace, however strained. Sharon offered Missionary Tisdale coffee and blueberry Danish before asking her if she had ever had Cous Cous. "I use codfish as my meat." "Danish is fine, Sister Edwards. I have a roast in the oven at the house." "Sharon please, Victoria. This is my home, not the church." Sharon was trying to be as diplomatic as she could in light of the circumstances. "I was relieved at finding out I'd found Cookies' underwear in Damon's room instead of that blond heifer that got him arrested. No, it's not the best situation for Andrea and Damon. Even so, we have to prepare ourselves to become grandmothers."

Victoria continued to pretend they weren't of the same ilk. Damon was going to have to make an honest woman of Cookie. Even though she would have chosen Malik, it was the right thing to do. Sharon, tired of Victoria's pontificating manner, decided it was time to put her in her place. "I'm going to say this the best way I know how," Sharon started. "Linford and I hold you and Samuel in very high esteem. The deacon is a very humble soul. You on the other hand, seem to think you are holier than Mary. I know you despise my son. He's no angel, but he is my child. Like it or not, Andrea came into my house of her own free will!" Missionary Tisdale sat stoically. With as much humility as she could muster she said, "Thank you, Sharon. I'm glad we understand each

other. Let us pray the children make the right decision."
Sharon sighed sympathetically. "It is you who needs prayer
– God has already worked this out." Both mothers through
how prophetic Sharon's statement was.

Damon spent the ten days following his arrest in jail.
Sharon reluctantly agreed it was time for him to realize he
couldn't continue to behave so callously. Walter Betancourt
met with the Edwards and offered to defend Damon, pro bono.
"No, this has nothing to do with one-upmanship. He may
have provoked K. D. into punching him but I don't believe
he intended to purchase the stiletto, or any other weapon for
that matter. He was an innocent victim of a stake-out by
E.C.P.D. This time his arrest was precipitated by my son's
assault on him. I owe you this much." Attorney Betancourt
argued for Damon as though he was defending Kadeem. He
proved his convictions about Damon's ignorance concerning
the hidden stiletto. As for the alcohol and trespassing
charges, misdemeanors, Damon was awarded 100 hours of
community service. These hours were to be completed before
he graduated from Marshall High. The first 30 hours were to
be completed monitoring the after-school recreation at Robert
E. Lee Christian Academy – the elementary school Little
Cameron attended. Civility. Humility. Integrity. The bad
blood was beginning to wash away.

NEW SHOES...BAD START

Damon's day in court was Monday, April third. Although he didn't fully understand why the father of his arch nemesis would defend him, he thanked Walter Betancourt for the brilliant argument he put forth on his behalf. As agreed, he returned to his parents' home, where a "minor" should be. After enduring yet another speech from his parents about a man handling his responsibilities, he half-heartedly approached Cookie about their dilemma. The sentence he prefaced his concern for Cookie and their child proved just how little sensitivity and wisdom he'd gained from his 10 day ordeal. "Yo, Cookie, my peeps say that we need to figure out what direction we're going to go with this baby." Cookie was calm. She wanted to give Damon the benefit of the doubt but he couldn't betray himself. She spoke soft and slow. "I'm not Shayla or Chereth, Damon. I never wanted nor will I ever want to be the mother of your child. My mother said 'a leopard can't change its spots.' In my heart I knew she was right, but she and I agreed, it was the right thing to do; to give you a chance. Listen to me well, Damon. My first mistake was to doubt myself and my friendship with Chenelle. My next mistake was to bless you with my innocence in order to prove my desire for men. The last mistake has already been fixed." She looked into his face for some emotion. Nothing. "It was all a bad April Fool's joke my brother," Cookie continued. "While you were sitting in jail Saturday, I took care of 'our' problem. I have places to go, things to see – I can't be tied down with a baby I don't want. Choices, Damon. I'm out!" The Demon seed was smote. She walked away with giving him a chance to counter attack.

Damon was confused. Was he feeling remorse for his lost child or was his ego bruised? Opt for the latter. Anyway, he sought Olivia out. She would understand his side. She would understand how unfairly he'd been treated. Olivia, however, didn't mince her words. "How can you stand there and say how unfair something is? Gamma told me what you told your mother about laying down with Shayla, Chelsea and Andrea." "Well, they say the apple don't fall far from the tree…" "Like father, like son? Don't even go there Damon. You're nothing like our father. Little Daddy was fourteen when he got my mother pregnant. You're a man – almost! Even though my grandparents refused to allow the Edwards to visit with me until I was teenager, our father never complained about getting a job and putting EVERY penny he earned away for me. 'Like father, like son,' please. You make me sick, Damon!"

Personal business aside, Cookie needed to get back in-stride with the team. Coaches Ashford and Forney never questioned her wish to be excused practice for a week. Coach Forney did warn her however, the day she returned wouldn't be a picnic. Stretches. Flights. Starts. Flights. Knee lifts. Flights. "Make that chin touch that knee Andrea. Your trail leg is too slow, and stop galloping between hurdles. I told you this week wasn't going to be nothing nice – didn't I?"

This was her bed of thorns. She wanted to hate somebody but couldn't. She almost regretted the tone she took with Damon when she spat out the word, "choices." Heike walked up to her as she sat down near the long jump pit. "Don't worry Cookie, Friday we're going to be smooth as silk." "I'm glad you think so girl! Hey, Keisha, tell your boy Geordi to take his foot out of my butt. He's killin' me!" Everybody went to Baskin-Robbins after practice – everyone except Cookie. She went home and went straight to bed.

It was mid – April. Everyone else was nearing perfection. 'Roni was flawless in the 100 and 200; focused on making the pilgrimage to Mecca – Tennessee State University. Keisha – Money! 'Tonya was great out of the blocks in the 4x100 MR and quick silver in the quarter. Chenelle was ever the cool anchor woman, a virtual wind-walker. Coach made Shamika Moss the permanent second leg of the 4x100 MR after she'd performed well during the week of Cookie's absence and the meet that followed. Cookie was out of sync in the hurdles, finishing no better than fourth place. It was time for a meeting of the inner circle.

Pooh's attempt at hitting the nail on the head brought things into partial focus. Her reunion with her father and blossoming relationship with Eric (Foots), turned her into a bundle of idealism. She showed the girls a picture of Cookie sitting beside a set of starting blocks, "See," she said. "She's looking at Malik in the stands instead of down the track. Girlfriend needs to get it together with her boy." "Get out Pooh," 'Roni teased. "Just because Foots got you trippin' doesn't mean Cookie's gone too." Nobody knew how right Pooh was, except Cookie. Not only did she need to get things right with Malik, she needed to come clean with her parents and God. Making amends with Malik wasn't as bad as Cookie anticipated. "I can get with your mixed feelings about leaving home as a virgin. Much love to you for not wanting to cause me to 'yield to temptation,' but why Damon?!" Paradox – familiar curiosity.

TISDALE'S STRENGTH

Samuel Tisdales' righteousness has been the meter stick for the saints of Mason Street A.M.E for ages. Their pastor had gone as far as nicknaming his Job-Abraham – his humility, the cornerstone of the church. When Cookie went to him asking if they could talk, she was more unnerved by his calm demeanor than the anticipation of his reaction to her sin. "Go get your mother Andrea. This is a family issue." "Yes, Daddy," she demurred. She would now gain an even stronger appreciation for the family values her father espoused. Colossians 3:18 -21 was the foundation upon which the Tisdale family was built;

18)"Wives, submit yourselves unto your own husbands, as it is fit in the Lord. 19) Husbands, love your wives, and be not bitter against them. 20) Children, obey your parents in all things; for this is well pleasing unto the Lord. 21) Fathers, provoke not your children to anger, lest they be discouraged."

When mother and daughter returned to the study, Samuel spoke. "God blessed me to be the head of this household some 35 years ago. Victoria, you have blessed me with seven children, four of them girls. I have seen you and each of the older girls 'with child' so I know the signs. Andrea, what is on your mind child?" "Cookie looked at Victoria first, then at Samuel. She searched his eyes, in awe of the silver-gray bands that encompassed the dark brown portals of compassion. Rings of the aged. Sagacious. He knew without knowing. Instead, she felt the warmth of her fathers' inner peace. Tranquility. She began to speak – freely. "Momma, before we even talked about what Damon and I should do about the 'problem,' it was done. I know I was carrying a life inside me but not even you knew what the future held for that baby. I made the choice I thought was best for everybody. Everyone is mad at Damon, but the truth is, I used him more than he used me. All I can do now is ask you and Daddy to forgive me for not telling you the truth from the beginning." Victoria sighed deeply. "Cookie, after I talked with Sharon, I had to get down off my high horse and onto my knees," Missionary Tisdale confessed. "It takes two to tango. I wish you had made a different decision but I have to respect the choice you've made. I need to be forgiven just as much as you do." Samuel nodded. Andrea had come of age. He opened his Bible and read two passages that, while they didn't condone Cookies' actions, they applauded her maturity. Metamorphosis.

I.(Colossians 3:12 – 14) 12) "Put on therefore, as the elect of God, holy and beloved bowels of mercies, kindness, humbleness of mind, meekness, long-suffering; 13) Forbearing one another, and forgiving one another, if any man have a quarrel against any: even as Christ forgave you , so also do ye. 14) And above all these things put on charity, which is the bond of prefectness."

II.(Phillipians 3:13 – 15) "…I count not myself to have apprehended: but this one thing I do, forgetting those things which are behind, and reaching forth unto those things which are before, 14) I press toward the mark for the prize of the high calling of God in Christ Jesus. 15) Let us therefore be thus minded: and if anything ye be otherwise minded, God shall reveal even this to you."

IT'S ABOUT TIME

Cookie had never been so enamored with her parents as she was now. She awoke Monday morning with a new found zeal that couldn't be shaken. Over the weekend the girls had appointed 'Roni to be the harbinger of bad tidings. 'Roni was very cautious in her tone during the ride to school. "Cookie, the coaches think you don't care about track anymore, but we know better. If you want to go to State with us, you've gotta' get busy. Heike is alright, but we made a pact girl." "I know. We never break a promise to the crew! You don't have to worry, this sista is ready to represent! Wait until this afternoon."

Heike and Keisha stood in the middle of the circle, leading calisthenics. Both were struck by Cookie's ebullience. "I hope that sister is ready. She needs to start bringing home some money!" "I heard you Keisha. You and Heike need to stop sweatin' me being quiet during exercise. Just be ready to watch my smoke when we run build-ups." "You go girl, talk that talk." "I'm going to walk the walk too, 'Roni. Like I told you on the way to school, I'm ready to represent. Heike, you're going to need more luck than that Frosch jacket today." "No you didn't just dis' my mom's college sweats," Heike joked. "I have never heard of Frosch College." "It's not a college. It's her maiden name." "Anyway…," Cookie sighed. Then she proceeded to prove she was back in-stride. BLOCKS. STRAIGHT-AWAYS. CURVES. BUILD-UPS. STRIDES. FLIGHTS. COOL DOWN. She didn't miss a step. "Geordi, Coach Ashford, this Friday, I'm going to own the hurdles; me and Heike, one and two!"

In addition to 'Roni's' letter from TSU, Keisha and Heike received letters from various schools offering track scholarships. "Listen up, listen up, listen up. I don't care who else sends me a letter, I'm going to Texas!," Keisha boast. "So sister girl, who are you signing with?" "I'm going to LSU. Cookie, are you coming with…?" "Heike, you're my girl and all that but track isn't my reality, sister. I'm off to see the world, I gotta dance." "Ladies," Coach Ashford interrupted. "Before we lace up our shoes and run off to college, we need to get through district, regional and state." "Okay, girls, let's come out of those sweats." "Aww, Geordi?," came the collective whine. "I never promised you it was going to be cake ladies." "Okay, Mr. Kinesiology. This is your show. We've got somewhere to go and it's time to get there!" "Well said, Miss Sapp. You want work, you got work. However, you are finished with the relays. I know about the letter from

TSU and the times Coach Cheesborough wants you to have – 11.3 in the 100 and 23.0 in the 200. It's on baby! And you Andrea, even though you're not going any further with track & field, for the next four days, you're going to eat, sleep and drink intermediates and lows (100 and 300)." "Have you bumped your head, Geordi? I've never run the 300M low hurdles." "Don't worry Andrea, this will be great for your dancing career!," Coach Forney laughed. "Whatever, Coach. You can't steal my joy!"

Tuesday afternoon Damon called Malcolm as he walked 'Roni out to practice. "Hey Tate, can I talk to you for a minute?" "What's up? I'm trying to watch my girl eat up some track!" "How many letters did you get?" "Six. One from Washington State, Ohio State, Florida State, Georgia Tech, University of Georgia (UGA), and the Gators. What about you?" "I only got one – from Clemson. I cant' go to Clemson man. That's where that hayseed is going!" "Maybe you need to talk to coach. Remember, he told you he wasn't going to help you lose your scholarship?" "True dat, Tate. True dat. I think I better go talk to that buster!" "Buster? Who are you to call someone a buster?," 'Roni interjected. "Let it go 'Roni. Cookie is over it, so everybody else should be too." "Over what Damon?" "You mean you didn't know?" Damon was surprised. He just knew Cookie shared everything with her quartet of friends. Already the source of enough confusion, he decided to leave well enough alone. "I'll holler at you later, Tate. 'Roni, you and your crew have a nice practice." "Talk to the hand, skeezer!" After Damon was gone, Malcolm looked at 'Roni angrily. "You didn't have to go there, 'Roni. The brother was trying to be humble." "Well, that's more than he deserves after all the harm he's done, especially to Shayla, Chenelle and Kadeem. I don't know why he brought Cookie's name into this conversation." When she asked Cookie at practice the answer never came. It was C-H-E-N-E-L-L-E's secret, as always. She got so angry, she ran 22.8 seconds, 22.7 seconds and 23.0 flat in the 200 and 11.2 seconds in each of the 100 meters she ran. "If you can do that next month, you can write your ticket to Tennessee," Coach Ashford encouraged. "You and the girls think Raimont, I mean Geordi, is such a taskmaster, but it was him who called Coach Cheesborough. Yea, he was dippin' as you girls call it. You'd be surprised at how much he pays attention to what you talk about while he's teaching you to run more efficiently!" The other half of the story behind the letter from Coach Cheesborough had come to light. She thought her mother was the only person who cared about her dream.

BAD TIMING

Friday morning Damon was still beside himself with grief. It was a travesty for him to have only received one scholarship offer. He stormed through the student parking lot in a blind rage. Seeing Mason and Chyna hand in hand, he yelled, "Yo Spawn, we need to talk!" "Look Damon, if you're going to get in my face about me dissin' you again, I ain't' trying to hear it!" "No on the real man. I need to know how many letters you got?" "Four or five, I can't remember right off." "From where?" "I know one is from Kansas and I think Colorado and 'Bama. Oh yeah, the last one is from Pitt." "Damn. Tate got six and you got four. We were the backbone of the defense and I only got one letter - From Clemson at that!" "Clemson's not a bad school..." "You know what I'm saying fool. ONE LETTER! That's where Hayseed from Franklin County is going." "I feel for you dude. Maybe you need to talk to coach." "That's the same B.S. Tate came at me with." Chyna started walking away. "You don't have to be Einstein to figure out if everyone is saying the same thing

then that's what you should do. Are you coming Mason?"
"Hold up Chyna. Check it out my brother. Later."

Coach Hawk was setting out the equipment for first period
P.E. when Damon stormed into the gymnasium. "Coach!,"
Damon yelled. "Wait, wait, wait; Mr. Edwards. You seem
to have forgotten yourself!" "I'm sorry, Coach. I want to
know why I only got one letter offering a football scholarship.
I busted my butt for you this year!" "You also got yourself
thrown out of the Homecoming dance. If it wasn't for your
being 'Demonseed', you would have been suspended for that
incident outside of Mr. Simone's class. You should be thankful
for that letter. No one else wants to take a chance on you now
that you've been arrested twice." Damon looked surprised.
"Oh, you didn't think I knew? Son, it's my business to know
about my players. Look, Clemson really wants Ashley Cannon
for their offensive line. For some reason I can't understand,
he won't sign unless they convince you to sign too. If you
want to play Damon, swallow your pride and go to Clemson.
I warned you but you wouldn't listen. You have no one to
blame except yourself. Well, there's the bell for first period.
Six bells later, after school…

"Okay girls, today is the last regular meet of the season. If
you do well; I'll call my sister and invite her to come to district
with us." "Come on Coach Ashford, this is serious," Tiffany
Ambrose chided. She was the choice to replace 'Roni as the
third leg of the 4x100 MR. "Relax tiffany. You'll do well.

This is just your tune-up for district in two weeks." "That's right girl. All you have to do is get me the baton within five yards of the leader – that is if you're not in the lead," Chenelle encouraged. "Yea, you don't want to be dissed on our home track!" "That's enough Keisha. She's under enough pressure as it is!," Coach Forney warned. "Okay Tiffany, if we draw lanes 2 or 3, your leg should be sweet. You just have to concentrate on not straying wide in the curve. Matter of fact, waltz on the inside line like it's a tight rope." "Good afternoon ladies and gentlemen. The lane assignments for today's 4x100 Meter relay are; East Crenshaw – lane 4, Taft-3, Morristown-2 and the Lady Panthers, lane 1." "Let's start this meet out right girls. Tiffany, you'll be running into the curve from the straight-away. Stay tight and don't get spooked by the stagger. Just get it to Chenelle and let her bring it home." "Okay Geordi," Tiffany said anxiously. He gave her an athletic pat on the butt. "How come I never get one of those?," Keisha teased. "Because you might like it, girlfriend," Cookie laughed before Coach Forney could respond. "You're a mess Keisha. Just bring me my money in the half mile!" Keisha started the Panther chant as the four relay teams walked out to their respective lanes.

"Runners take your mark, get set, CRRACK." Tonya sprang from the blocks just as quick as the guns' retort and smoke dissipated into the breeze. She hugged the inside line tight and consummated a smooth right to left hand exchange with Shamika. "TACA-TACA-TACA-TACA," was the smooth gliding cadence Tiffany heard bearing down on her. She was standing on the wrong side of the lane to receive a left to right hand exchange which caused Shamika to break stride in order to affect an exchange without calamity. "You go girl," Shamika yelled and Tiffany was off. Coach Forney's advice raced through her head. "Don't get spooked by the stagger, waltz the line." "Come on Tiffany, bring me the baton sister!," Chenelle yelled. All Tiffany could focus on was Ebony Morris in lane 4. Like her brother Lavell, she was East Crenshaw's speed merchant. Spooked by the stagger. Ebony was practically in the straight-away when Tiffany yelled to Chenelle, "You go girl!" "Whoop, whoop, whoop, look at my sister!," Kenyan yelled. "She is BAD!!!" The Marshall crowd joined in. "Whoop, whoop, whoop!;" the walk was on. Gotta save face on home turf. Ebony leaned. Chenelle leaned further. Red flag in the curve signaling a disqualification. Tiffany had not completely relinquished her grip on the baton before Chenelle exited the exchange zone. "I'm sorry Chenelle," Tiffany offered. "Ain't no pressure sister girl. Ebony knows she got walked today!" Still dejected, Tiffany walked over to Coach Ashford and apologized. "Today was to work out the butterflies. You'll be fine at Regionals. The Lady Panthers lost the 4x100MR battle but won the "war" by 20 points.

IT'S ALL COMING TOGETHER

Everyone's dreams were coming to life – receiving scholarship offers for their respective sports. 'Tonya arrived home after the meet to be greeted at the door by her father, Bernard, a retired Marine Corps Gunnery Sergeant. He was the proud bearer of a Silver Star and two Purple Hearts – awarded for leading a patrol which extracted a downed helicopter crew from behind enemy lines during his tour in Vietnam. Bernard handed 'Tonya two letters. She'd been worried about her acceptance to the Air Force Academy since failing that physics test during basketball season -wasted worry. In addition to her high SAT's, his Silver Star and two Purple Hearts were the bonus chips that assured her acceptance. There was also an offer to play basketball for UGA. Basketball was her passion, engineering was he dream. She chose the Academy. That burden off her shoulders, she could put her focus on better things – the prom and regionals, not necessarily in that order.

Even though the prom was after state, it was time to start shopping for the material and notions. First Sunday was Mother's Appreciation Day. The girls planned to treat their mothers to lunch and then announce to Miss Nona she'd been nominated to be their seamstress. "Momma…, 'Roni, 'Tonya, Cookie and Pooh liked the dresses you made for the Tom Thumb wedding and our sixth grade graduation so much that they want you to make their dresses for the Prom. "Please, Miss Nona," the girls begged. "We've been waiting six years for this." Nona looked into their puppy-eyed faces and laughed. "You know you don't have to look so pitiful. I would have been upset if you didn't ask me!" The girls bum rushed her – bathing her with kisses. "Oh, go away. You know how I feel about them ole Judas kisses." "But we really do love you Miss Nona," the girls sang.

Page and Talley were spearheading the Senior Class play. The one talent they lacked however was choreography. They went to Miss Bennett for advice. When she responded, "Ask Andrea Tisdale to help you," they couldn't mask their embarrassment. "Duh," Page said. "Why didn't we think of that Talley?" "Just dumb I guess. Thanks Miss Bennett. We'll try to catch up with her at lunch time." They found Cookie and company sitting at their usual table. "Andrea, we have an offer you can't refuse," Talley joked. "And?" "And for the mere price of the answer 'yes', we'll let you dance in the senior class play." "What is it?" "Did you ever watch Fame when you were younger?" "Girlfriend, I thought I was Debbie Allen's alter ego. You don't know how many times I fell on my butt trying to move like her." "Then you'll do it?!," Page asked. "Of course, but you have to answer one question for me." "What's that?" "Do you really have tattoo of Tinkerbell on your poonie?" Embarrassed, Page looked at Chenelle and said, "Anyway!" "Meet us at Pizza Hut tonight and we'll tell you what to do," Talley said.

"You know you're wrong for that Cookie!," Chenelle chided as Talley and Page walked away. "Talley didn't know that secret!" "I hate it for her," Cookie laughed. "Does anybody know what Coach has planned for practice today?" "Blocks and exchanges," 'Roni sighed. "Geordi wants to win the relays hands down! He also said if anybody false starts he'll kill 'em."

"Keisha, circle everybody for calisthenics. Veronica, hand out these work-out sheets while Coach Forney tells you what we expect to accomplish over the next two weeks." "Okay ladies, here it is. As you know; only the top two finishers in each event advance to the next level. You girls in the sprints have to be focused from the blocks through the tape. In the distance events you can't get boxed in or you're dead. Keisha, you need to get under 2 minutes 15 seconds this week! In the relays, please ladies, make sure you KNOW WHERE THE

ZONE BEGINS AND ENDS. We want these relays!" "Yes
we do!," Coach Ashford said emphatically. These will be the
teams:

The 4 x 100	The 4 x 400
LaTonya	Tramaine Lovett
Shamika	Amber Forbes
Tiffany	Keisha
Chenelle	LaTonya
with Beth Waite	with Latifah Battle
and Ciara Greene	and Sean Hale
as alternates	as alternates

Okay, Veronica, Heike, Andrea, 'Tonya and Tramaine;
let's work on those starts. It's a fine line between false starting
and getting left in the blocks."

Coach Ashford concentrated on the girls in the field events
while Geordi worked on the blocks – taking an occasional
glance at the distance runners. Keisha seemed to be dogging
it on the first lap of the mile jog he'd assigned as a warm-
up. "Come on Keisha," he yelled as she began the second
lap. "You still have three laps plus a quarter and a 200 at
50-75% before I put you on the clock!" "I'm doing my best
Geordi," Keisha snarled. "Yea?, and I'm Lonnie Lunchmeat
too! What's up Keisha!" "I said I'm doing my best! You try

jogging a mile without proper support Mister!" "Oh, but I have," Geordi laughed. "Oh but I have. I was a 200/400 man in college. I'll forgive you today but have your package tight tomorrow. Are we her, Miss Money?" "I feel you Coach," Keisha answered with a devilish grin. "Oh no you don't, Miss Lady!," Coach Ashford interjected. "Valkyrie Sports donated an assortment of sports bras this year in exchange for advertisement space in the yearbook and sports booklets. I'm sure we have one in your size." "I didn't know you had a PHD (Player Hater Degree) Coach!" "I don't need a PhD to leave you here when the bus pulls out either, sister! If I were you, I would carry my self and my smart mouth to the locker room and 'handle my business' as you are so fond of saying."

"I guess you told me, didn't you'" Keisha laughed trying to hide her embarrassment. "A sister's gotta do what she's gotta do. It's never personal, just about the 'money'," Coach winked. Keisha winked back, acknowledging Coach Ashford's humorous attempt at taking the sting out of her admonishment. She and the equipment manager ran to the gym, "handled her business," and returned to practice with new found vigor. Geordi put her on the clock.

CHUMP CHANGE

"Keisha, line up in lane 3; Tramaine and Amber, lanes 1 and 2. Run the first quarter at about 70- 72 seconds. 'Tonya, Sean and Latifah pick her up at the start of the second quarter and push her to the limit. I want my money, Keisha!"

Tramaine was already in the zone, warm from a good series of starts. Both she and Amber blew through the curve breaking the stagger even with Keisha. Amber led down the back stretch with Tramaine and Keisha close behind, struggling to stay in the 70-72 second range. "I gotta get somewhere Girl," Keisha yelled, inciting the two quarter milers to quicken the pace. Tramaine opened it up in the bottom and down the front, bringing them through at 65, 65.3 and 68. "Looking good, Keisha. Don't get boxed by this second group." But that was the plan.

'Tonya, Sean and Latifah fell around her like a swarm of bees, forcing her to run the first curve of the second quarter on the rail. If she slowed her pace in order to step into the second lane, Sean laid on her shoulder. When she sped up, 'Tonya slowed down. Finally, with 150 yards to run, Keisha sensed a slight opening and challenged 'Tonya to hold her off. 'Tonya allowed Keisha to finish a step ahead of her. Delighted, Keisha yelled, "Cha-ching," throwing her arms into the air victoriously. "Please, Keisha. 2:18 is three seconds too slow!," Coach Forney teased. "I know you told them to trap me!" "And? Don't you think the rest of the coaches in the state are telling their girls to do the same thing?! You are ranked in the top five in the state, young lady – on paper that is. You cant' prove it if you don't get there. That's when you can say 'Cha-ching!'"

Cookie noticed Kadeem standing near the high jump mat and began to panic. "Chenelle, aren't you coming with me to Pizza Hut?" "What's the matter, Cookie, you think Page is going to get you back for busting her out at lunch time?," 'Roni teased. "Who? She better recognize. I just don't want to sit with them very long." "Well, call Malik and tell him to meet you there. I'm going to a dinner party with Kadeem and his family." "Oh excuse me, Miss Bourgeois!" "It's not even like that Cookie. Some of his father's frat boys are in town for a twenty-year get together at the Marriot. His moms thought it would be nice if I came along since one of them is a Political Science professor at Howard." "Did you guys forget about Pooh's skate party?," 'Tonya asked. "Thank you Girl. That's my way out of going to Pizza Hut. You know you're wrong Cookie. 'Gw'on over there and make us proud,' Little Miss Debbie Allen," Chenelle laughed. Cookie raised an opened hand toward the girls. "Y'all know what to do." "Yea, meet you at the skate rink after you finish your business with Page and Talley," Chenelle answered as everyone else broke into laughter.

Cookie's real reason for not wanting to go alone was the foreboding feeling she got each time she remembered the conversation she and Chyna had in that very same pizza parlor. After a little introspection, she concluded it was the conversation and its aftermath, instead of the place that gave rise to the foreboding. She called Malik and told him to meet her at the infamous Pizza Hut in an hour.

FALLING LIKE DOMINOES

Malik met Cookie at Pizza Hut as planned. "We are going to Pooh's skate party, right?" "Yea, after you follow me home so I can give Momma her car." "We ain't gone yet?," Malik joked.

Pooh and Foots met them before they got to the check-out counter. "Don't get any skates," Pooh said. "We already got an 8 for Cookie and a 10, 11, and 12 for your boats, my brother," she laughed. "Well, at least they're not as big as his foots are sister," Malik joked in return. "Chenelle and Kadeem said they wouldn't stay at his pops party long so they should be here soon. We know how you seem lost without her," 'Roni chimed. "Don't start with me Miss Thing. I don't need anybody except my Boo," Cookie laughed. Malik beat his chest and grinned. "Yea!" Chenelle and Kadeem arrived twenty minutes later, proclaiming, "Marshall High in the house!"

Couples skate. Line skate. Speed skate. Girls skate. Guys skate. Backward skate. Fancy skate. Malik was Gregory Hines on wheels. Unfortunately, the less adept skaters are encouraged to test their skills at the same time. As Malik was spinning around to skate backwards, an out-of-control skater blind-sided him causing their skates to become entangled. A chain reaction began until the skaters were sprawled across the floor. Insult to injury – Malik broke his right pinky finger. "Remember when you were joking about Malik clowning when you asked him to carry your books, girlfriend? Let's see who clowns now," Chenelle teased. The out-of –control skater attended East Crenshaw High. Payback.

Regionals. "Okay girls; tell you boyfriends you'll see them when you get back. We've got a region to outrun. No butterflies, jitters or ghosts. How are you feeling Tiffany?" "I'm your girl, Geordi. 24-7." "Don't be trying to steal my man, Little Miss Ambrose. He don't need your honey when I'm giving him the money!" "You're so stoopid Keisha. You can have him if you let me listen to your MC Lyte tape." "I don't think so sista. I need to get into the zone before we get to Morristown." "Too much drama for me," Tiffany laughed. "I'll just listen to Queen Latifah." The spectrum of colors at Morristown was as spectacular as it was at the St. Julius/St. Patrick's Invitational. "Tiffany, this is a lot bigger than the quad-meet last week. Preliminaries and finals. Twice the drama." "Step off Keisha," Tiffany smiled. "I'm on top of my game. Ciara and I have been practicing at the middle school around the corner from her house. Watch me."

Last call for the 400 Meter Relay. "Alright Tiffany, show time. Remember what we worked on. Twelve steps before the zone line…," Ciara reminded Tiffany. Tiffany paced off twelve steps and marked the spot with one strip of purple tape crossed by one strip of yellow. "You go girl," and Tiffany was off. The baton exchange with Chenelle was fluid. Chenelle maintained the five meter lead, coasting across the finish line at 49.6 seconds flat. Finals were better – 48.7 seconds. On the way to state with East Crenshaw in tow – 49.2 seconds.

Ciara had an agenda of her own – winning the 100 meter dash. "Coach, I'm going to win the 100. I want to be more than just the first alternate for the relay team." "I admire your confidence, Ciara," Coach Ashford offered. "I'm sure Veronica will welcome the competition." "This is about Ciara Greene, not Veronica Sapp, Coach!" "I'm sorry, Ciara. I didn't think you were serious. What have we got to lose?" "Nathan!" Nothing indeed. Ciara won her heat easily. So did 'Roni and Ebony Morris. "Aren't you tired of seeing Purple, Gold and Black, yet girlfriend?," 'Roni asked Ebony. "That was the relay – this is the 100 meters." "But you know this is my race and has been all season." "Anyway!," Ebony said, tiring of the banter, "this is the tie breaker for us. I'm fixin' to break you off some!" Both 'Roni and Ebony discounted the aspirations of the six other contestants in the finals section. "Good luck 'Roni," Ciara said. "Okay, girl, see you on the other end."

No false starts. The race began to take shape at 40 meters with Lacey Watts of Morristown holding a slight lead in lane 6. Ebony and 'Roni were stride for stride in lanes 3 and 4. No one was focused on lane 1. At 70 meters, Ebony and 'Roni were still stride for stride, however, they led the field as expected. "Coach, look at Ciara. She's walking 'Roni and Ebony down." "I don't believe it. She said she was going to win it." Ciara held true to her prediction, out leaning 'Roni at the tape – 11.5, 11.505, 11.51. 'Roni raised Ciara's hand into the air triumphantly. Panthers first and second. "I gotta give you props sista. I didn't think you could get me," 'Roni confessed between breaths as they walked back to the finish line. "I didn't want to just be part of the team. I wanted to be one of the money makers." "Hey Ebony, two out of three. I hate it for you. You just got served up on the one tip so you're finished except for the relay – which finished second to us. My girl won today but the 100 is mine at state – what do you think abut that, Ciara?" Ciara just smiled and raised both arms above her head. It was going to be a good day. Everyone else advanced in their respective events as expected. REGIONAL CHAMPIONS.

Coach Ashford was so elated she couldn't contain herself. After eight years as Head Coach of the Bradford, now Marshall Panther's girls track team, she'd finally won a regional championship. After accepting the trophy, she started the chant. "Listen up, listen up, listen up…" Keisha looked at her and winked. "I know Coach; a sista's gotta do what a sista's gotta do. If you were any body else, I'd be upset." The team joined in. "Panthers, Panthers, Purple and Gold, we are swift, we are bold. You go girl!"

Tiffany was concerned Ciara's stunning performance was being over-shadowed by the championship hoopla. After everyone had gotten on the bus she broached the subject of the Nike statuette. "Hey Coach?, who gets the trophy today?" "You don't know?," Shamika laughed in disbelief. To everyone else it was a foregone conclusion. On cue, Keisha stood in the aisle. "Today's nominees for the coveted Nike statuette are"

1) For their usual one/two finish in the hurdles…Heike and Andrea

2) For her usual first place finish in the 800…Keisha

3) For her usual first place finish in the 200…'Roni

4) For her stunning walk down of 'Roni and Ebony… Ciara

And the winner is?" Latifah mockingly opened the envelope but was interrupted before she could announce the winner. "Ain't no drama. After walking me down like that today, Ciara's got to be the winner," 'Roni said. "You got down today girl and I got nothing but love for you. But like I told Ebony, state belongs to me!" Coach Ashford confirmed the girls' speculation saying, "Thanks for the theatrics ladies – Ciara is today's heroine. Go to sleep. Today is history, next week – STATE.

In addition to Ciara's upset victory, the Panthers went one and two in the quarter, placed second in the high jump, long jump and one/two in the 200. Since state was a three day evolution, Coach Ashford's focus was again on the fine points of each event – technique and endurance. "This is a short week of practice girls. As we saw last week with Ciara's win, nothing is etched in stone. Stay focused from start to finish. Make sure you have your steps down on the runway in the long and high jumps. Fall forward and keep your butt off the bar." "Make sure you have all your 'necessary gear' please," Geordi added. "So, what are you tryin' to say, Coach," Keisha laughed. "Then we're here, right?" "Right!"

During lunch Wednesday, 'Roni announced she had a surprise. "Last night when Malcolm and I were at the mall I saw this offer far a free pair of earrings with a body piercing, no matter what you have pierced." "I don't know about you, girl," 'Tonya said with a hint of apprehension in her voice. "No, silly, it ain't even like that. I figure if we all get our nose pierced..." "Oooh. That would be tight to death," Chenelle agreed. By the end of the day the whole team heard and approved of 'Roni's idea. "What side and what kind of earrings are we going to get?," Heike asked. "Black Onyx on the right side!," 'Roni announced emphatically. Finally, something everybody agreed on. State was definitely the time to shine.

Thursday morning, 6:00 am. - Time to board the chartered Greyhound – a gift from Micah Henderson. He was the owner/manager of the Bradford Bus Depot – twenty-five years of faithful, zealous service. The girls would be comfortable on the ride to State. After ensuring the school banner was affixed to the outside of the bus, Geordi shook hands with Micah. "Thank Greyhound for us, Sir." "No, Greyhound thanks you, Mr. Forney. You've done a great job with these girls." They shook hands once more before Geordi got on the bus. It would be a six-hour ride to the site of the state meet.

"Etienne, I want to thank you for bringing me onboard this season. I hope I've accomplished everything you asked me to." "Are you kidding? The regional championship last week was MORE than I'd hoped for! If you didn't, those eyes did," she joked. "Raimont, for the last two seasons I've been trying to get Keisha to be serious about this thing. Veronica is a natural on the track. 'Tonya, Andrea and Chenelle just make her more relaxed." "I heard they've been best friends since second grade." "You're right. Friendship is the catalyst. Their strength is our nucleus. They made a pact to do one last thing together before graduation. Fortunately for us, they chose Track and Field."

After settling into the hotel and having a light lunch, Coach herded the girls onto the bus so they could go over to the stadium and get a good look at the track – chase the demons away. "This is the bomb!," Pooh said. Pooh and Quinn Apple, sports writer for the school paper, were allowed to travel with the team - this being the schools' largest representation at the state level. Although St. Julius was only twenty miles from Bradford, they were in a different region. The rivalry was already set with Lana Mullis determined to get her revenge. She sought Cookie out after the opening ceremonies to offer a friendly challenge but ran into Heike first.

"That's a pretty ponytail you're wearing, Lana but you're 'knot' at the right party!," Heike laughed, stroking her own coif for emphasis. You're kinda cute yourself but I prefer to let my race do the talking," Lana answered curtly. "When the final race is over the announcer is going to say, 'will the real Salt-n-Pepa please stand'. Don't bother coming over to the podium. It's going to be me and Cookie." "That's Andrea to you!," Cookie said, as she walked over to the warm-up area. "Are you dissin' me in front of company again girlfriend?" "Oh, no, you know you're my girl. I was talking to Lana. It's Marshall High all the way, me and you, one and two!" They looked at Lana struggling to stay composed. "I was trying to be a sport about this," she said. "We hate it for you, but somebody's go to lose," Cookie finished. Pre-lims. Each qualified handily. First day was over for Heike and Lana.

Cookie still had the 300 lows to run. Save the drama…the Lady Panthers showed their tails Thursday night.

With the exception of 'Tonya in the high jump, and Cookie, in the long jump; Friday was a free day. Nevertheless, Etienne mustered the gang at 8:00 O'clock for a light breakfast and proceeded to the stadium for a mini-workout. The long jump was scheduled to begin at 10:30. "Pooh, make sure you get me right as I hit the board," Cookie said. "I'm going to win Marshall High's first medal this weekend." "I wouldn't be too sure, Cookie. You know Miss Thing from St. Julius said she was going to beat you even if she has to jump out of the pit," Heike laughed. "Well she better call JJK (Jackie Joyner-Kersee) and ask if she can borrow her legs 'cause you know I got mad skills!" "You need to stop girl," Chenelle cautioned. In one ear and out the other - Cookie cast fate to the wind.

Lana was awarded the privilege of jumping last in the finals since she had the best qualifying leap. "Andrea Tisdale, Marshall High Panthers, jumping seventh." The distance to beat was 17 feet 2 inches. Cookie felt the pressure immediately. "See it, hear it, and do it!" Cookie bolted down the runway visualizing the spot where she wanted to land. She heard each step then her launch foot struck the board. "Windmill, plant, and hop forward." She lost a foot falling backward. Lana leapt that foot plus six inches, 17' 6". She then walked out of the pit, brushed the sand off her leg and made a gesture in Cookie's direction implying her butt was too big. Whether or not it was her intention to cause Cookie to loose her focus, she did just that. On the next two leaps, Cookie scratched the first and aborted the second. Lana now led to competition by four inches.

Once again Cookie played back Coach Ashford's instructions in her mind. "Pooh, get the camera. Andrea is representing!" She changed her routine before starting down the runway. SQUAT. STAND-UP. ROCK BACK ON YOUR HEELS. PERFECT SPRINT. PLANT. WINDMILL. HIT. HOP FORWARD. PERFECT JUMP. "Your four and more!," Cookie yelled.

17' 10" – a short lived victory. Winona Broward of Franklin leapt 17' 10 ¾ inches, raising the ante. "Cookie is at least guaranteed second place," 'Tonya said. "Yea, my girl is going to win Marshall's first medal just like she said," Heike chimed in. Chenelle, 'Tonya, 'Roni and Heike held hands prayerfully as Lana stood poised for her final leap.

"The jump is clean," yelled the line official. "17 feet 11 inches!" Air (heir) apparent. Lana surpassed Winona by ¼ of an inch. Cookie was out of the medals. She looked at Lana and Winona congratulating each other and smiled. "I hate it for you," she whispered much to her chagrin – remembering the cattiness she and Heike had subjected Lana to last night. "It's up to you 'Tonya," Cookie said. "I know you ain't feeling sorry for yourself, Girlfriend." "You weren't the one who just got served up!" "Save the drama Cookie. You and Heike will get her tomorrow!" "And?!" "And you know you really want me to win the first medal anyway," 'Tonya joked. Ironically, she got a charley horse in her right thigh and couldn't make height. The lesson of the day – there's always tomorrow.

"So Geordi, are we still going to dinner tonight?," Keisha joked as the team left the stadium. On cue, Ciara grabbed his arm and said, "The only way he goes to dinner with you is if I get to listen to MC Lyte!" "Ladies, ladies, I don't think Mrs. Forney is willing to share me with any one except our sons. In fact, she'll be here to meet us at the hotel at about 6' 0'clock this evening." "A sista can't have no fun, can she?!," Keisha pretended to pout. Ciara gave her a high five while saying, "I didn't want to listen to your tape anyway!" "Your new names are 'Trip One and Trip two," Tiffany said. "You need to be thinking about that 800 and 100 tomorrow." "Oh, and you're not worried about the 4 x 100?," Ciara teased. "No, no, no!," Shamika said emphatically. "And why not?" "You mean you don't know, Ciara? Well, you better ask somebody!" "So why aren't you scared?," Keisha chimed in. Shamika, Tiffany, and 'Tonya pointed at Chenelle. "Because NOBODY escapes THE QUEEN!," 'Tonya announced. "Let's not count our chickens before they hatch," Coach Ashford cautioned. "See, there you go player hating again, Coach." "Keisha…" "We're just tryin' to have some fun Coach." "Okay. Maybe I should loosen up some. Listen. We're going to treat you all to Red Lobster tonight but you have to be on your best behavior." "Girls, you are ambassadors for Thurgood Marshall High…,"

Cookie said mockingly. "Andrea, you and Keisha are a regular 'Laverne and Shirley.' You should get your own stand-up routine after graduation." "Laverne and who?" "I forgot – that's before your time." "You didn't have to go there Coach," Cookie laughed.

The Lady Panthers sat down to dinner at 7:00 pm. Geordi remained at the hotel, anxiously waiting for his family. After thirty minutes he breathed a sigh of relief as his eggplant purple Explorer pulled under the awning, finally. "I thought you'd never get here." "You know Bad and Badder have to stop at every gas station we see. I could tell you where every Amoco between here and Bradford are. Look at the back seat! They had to see who's soda could spray highest." "Fellas, I thought I told you not to sweat Mommy so hard?" Five year-old terrors. "It was him, Daddy." "Nah, ahw, it was him." "Alright, you keep clowning and I'm going to get in your back pockets. Understand?!" The twins nodded – scowling at each other. "Wash up so I can get you over to Red Lobster to meet the team."

Pooh was the first to notice Geordi and family being ushered to the rear of the restaurant amidst the cacophony of girlish chatter. "Well, isn't this a Kodak Moment, Quinn? Freeze, Geordi, I can't pass up this photo opportunity." "Girls, this is my wife, Elise, and my two terrors, Ramon and Damon." A hush fell over the table 'Roni, Chenelle, Cookie, 'Tonya and Heike shared. "No they didn't curse

217

that baby like that," Heike whispered. "I feel you girlfriend," 'Roni agreed. The name Damon – salt in a festering wound. "Speaking of Damon…" 'Roni started. "Malcolm and Malik are just as tight as you and Chenelle, Cookie. When Malcolm and I were picking out these earrings, he told me what Malik said; 'at least your girl doesn't have your parents doubting you.' What did you and Damon do that almost caused Malik and Malcolm to fight each other that day Damon went to jail?" "I don't want to talk about it now." "I think you don't want to tell us." "I bet Chenelle knows!," 'Tonya added. "It's always you and Chenelle. We promised not to keep secrets from each other when we were little, remember? But, every since sixth grade, me, 'Tonya and Pooh have been left out of a lot of secrets and it's not right." Chenelle broke her silence.

"Cookie is right and, so are you. This isn't the time or place to talk about that." "So when, then?, " 'Tonya asked. "And don't say when we get home either. Davenport Bridge isn't the only place we can talk." "When we get back to the hotel," Cookie conceded. Damon had been the cause of many of the secret traumas each had suffered, directly and indirectly, over the last ten years. In room 247, Howard Johnson's Hotel, Cookie had the last word before lights out. "Remember the rumor Cherry kept up about Shayla? Well, if she would have put my name in it, it would have been true."

DAY OF RECKONING

Cookie was the first to awaken Saturday morning. 5' O'clock am. Not wanting to disturb any one else, she tiptoed into the bathroom and sat in the tub – pulling the shower curtain. Pooh, who was sharing the adjoining room (246) with Heike, Quinn, and Keisha, found she couldn't sleep either. Her heart was still heavy with the revelation of Chenelle and Cookie's ordeal. She woke Heike, coaxing her to knock on the connecting door to awaken the rest of the Davenport girls. 'Tonya unlocked the door, fussing. "Have you bumped your head, Heike?" "It's not her fault," Pooh confessed. "I asked her to knock on the door. After last night girl, I think we need to pray for you guys to have clear heads and consciences." 'Tonya looked at Pooh in disbelief. "Pooh...?" "No really! I know you all prayed for me when my daddy came home. Chenelle and Cookie have been holding onto that junk for a long time and we've been mad at them just as long. Now that it's all out, we need to give it up." "I was cool last night when Cookie turned the light out." "Where is she anyway?" "I'm in the bath tub talking to the walls because I didn't want to wake anybody up, Pooh." "I'm sorry, but I couldn't sleep any longer...," "I heard you telling 'Tonya. If I didn't think you were right sista, you'd be getting sounded on right about now." "See, I knew you still had a lot on your heart."

Heike and Pooh crossed through the portal, locking the door behind them. Keisha and Quinn weren't even roused. "Okay Pooh," 'Roni said, stretching. "It's your idea so you start the prayer." "I ain't shame, 'Roni. I don't know if you realize it or not, this is the last thing we do together as students – except graduation." "We...?" "Yes, we. I'm not running but I'm here with you. Anyway, Damon has pained us since second grade in one way or another. You guys don't need any more drama than what's gonna happen on the track today. Besides, if you don't look good, I don't get good pictures." "You know you're wrong for that, Pooh," Chenelle laughed. "You need to go ahead and pray girl so I can go back to sleep!," 'Tonya said. "I'm going to be the first one on the track, remember. I can't be sleeping when that gun goes off." "Talk to the hand silly," Pooh jested – then she started to pray.

Déjà vu'. With the exception of asking for strength to forgive Damon, Coach Ashford's prayer was virtually Pooh's, verbatim. "..., And Father, God, please keep these sisters free from injury today, free and focused." "I thought you were Catholic, Etienne?," Geordie teased. "You prayed like a Baptist bishop, sister." "Like Keisha says, 'a sista's gotta do…'" "Nia, (team manager) read the order of events please. Ladies, don't get caught out there, not paying attention to the announcement of your race. Many a gold medal has been lost because Olympians weren't focused."

12:15 pm Opening Ceremonies

1:15 pm 400 Meter Relay

1:20 pm 400 Meter Dash

1:40 pm 100 Meter Dash

2:05 pm 100 Meter Intermediate Hurdles

2:30 pm 800 Meter Run

3:00 pm 200 Meter Dash

3:35 pm 300 Meter Low Hurdles

4:05 pm 1600 Meter Relay

4:35 pm Presentation of Trophies

"Last call for the 4 x 100 MR." " 'Tonya, check your spikes and stay loose in the blocks." "Chill, Geordi. I'm 'bout it, 'bout it. Gwen Torrance can't get with me today!" "Talk that talk but will you walk the walk?" "That's what we have Chenelle for – like you didn't know!" No one noticed the busloads of Marshall High parents entering the stands.

However, it wasn't long before Micah made their presence known.

The girls drew lane 1. They knew from the beginning, they'd have to slay dragons. East Crenshaw, lane 5, had a chip on their shoulders from the regional defeat. Albany Metropolitan, lane 3, fielded a relay with each girl said to run 11.8 on a bad day – guaranteed to go sub 48 seconds. And, in lane 4, the defending state champions, Springfield Gazelles boasted there wasn't another 4 x 100MR team in the state that could match the talent of Napthali and Saida Bramble, nicknamed Grace and Poetry. Napthali was a junior, Saida, a senior. "Ladies, walk to your positions." "Who you with?," Shamika asked. "Panthers, 24-7, you go girl!," was the collective response. They each rubbed the onyx post in their nose and jogged to their positions.

"Runners take your marks – Set – POW!" 'Tonya rose to the level of competition immediately. Her split was 11.6 seconds, taking a slight lead over the stagger. Shamika ran wide, nearly drifting into lane 2 and had to break stride. She ran 12.0. The stagger was even again. "Come on Tiffany. Go get her!,' Ciara yelled. Napthali blazed an 11.63 split, pulling away from the field. Tiffany ran a valiant 11.9 seconds. The Gazelles had center stage. Chenelle saw Tiffany hit her mark. She listened for the patented, "You go girl," but heard, "Come on Baby girl!," instead. Quicksilver, she ran a stunning 11.59, finishing a stride ahead of Saida. Saida's split

– 11.61. Drama. Panthers – 47.09 seconds, Gazelles – 47.11; Albany Metro – 47.12. Chenelle raised her teammate's arms triumphantly and bowed toward the stands. It was on.

Marshall High drew "first blood" but Springfield wasn't to be denied. Tramaine and Amber were soon to understand why Napthali was called Grace. The 57.1 seconds quarter she'd run during pre-lims lulled them into a false since of security, having run 56.4 and 56.5 respectively. From lanes three and four, Tramaine and Amber led the field through the first 200 at 27 seconds. Napthali was fluid out in lane 8, coming through at 29. Tramaine and Amber came through the 300 at 40, Napthali at 42. The she hit warp – sucking everyone into the vortex. "Ladies and Gentlemen, Napthali Bramble of the Springfield Gazelles with a new meet and state record – 53.6 seconds." Tramaine ran 54.6 and Amber, 54.8. "I don't know if I can do this for the rest of the day, Raimont." "I know what you're saying, Etienne. Tramaine and Amber break 55 seconds and finish second and third. The Gazelles didn't come to play."

The Old heads sat in the stands talking amongst themselves, hoping their Panthers could maintain their slight lead (total points) over the Gazelles. Pride in the accomplishments of the children allows parents to recapture their youth – vicarious living. Back in the day it was called "joning, playing the dozens and talkin' trash." Then and now, the gist was jest – poke fun while giving respect to the better "player." Gabriel

"Popeye" Bramble sat to their right. "Whew, that little girl is bad." "Yes she is, Sapp," Micah agreed. "That's my 'bad' little girl, Sir," Gabriel boasted. "I guess the young lady who anchored the Panthers' relay is your daughter?," he asked Micah. "That's me," Micah beamed. "That was smooth how she walked my big girl, Saida." "That's why they call her the Queen." "The relay was just her warm-up. You see what my baby just did in the open 400? Saida is just as nice in the 200." "Then you want to talk to Sapp about the outcome of that race." "Sapp? That's the right name for an also ran," Gabriel laughed. "What's your name, my brother?" "Gabriel, but you can call me Popeye." "Well, Good Brother, when the gun goes off I want you to stand up and do that dance we used to do back in the day and watch my baby run that 23 point. Tennessee State can't wait for her to graduate. Where is you girl going after she loses to another Panther?" "Florida. Well, we have about an hour before we see who's daughter is truly the baddest, Sapp." "Not really, Popeye. 'Roni is getting ready to show you why you should be glad she wasn't the anchor of the relay." "Last call for the 100 meter dash," was announced. "Good luck in the 200, Popeye. This 100 meters is in the bag!"

"I'll see you at the other end, Ciara." "Okay 'Roni. Me and you – one and two." Unfortunately, Ciara couldn't rise to the level of competition. She duplicated her regional performance of 11.5. 'Roni ran 11.38. Albany Metro 11.47. Sapp turned and pointed at Bramble. "Did you see that Popeye?" "She is bad, Sapp, but I gotta stay with mine." "Like the New Jacks say, 'I hate it for ya." The two fathers shook hands. One hour until showdown.

...IN THE MEANTIME...

"Last call for the 100M IH final." "Okay, Salt-n-Pepa. It's Showtime. Cookie, no slacking. Even though you have the 300's later, you still need to give all you've got now. You and Heike have been a tandem to deal with most of the season. Heike, you have lane 3 and Cookie, lane 5. You guessed it – Lana is in 4. Stay loose in the blocks and remember..." "We know, it's a fine line between a false start and getting left in the blocks."

"Runners take your marks, set..." False start Albany Metro, in lane 6. Again. False start Springfield, in lane 1. "Stay loose," Coach Forney yelled. Heike and Cookie were focused. "Pow!" The three center lanes seemed to meld into one. For eighty meters the staccato cadences of the three individuals were indistinguishable. Sough virtuosity. "Come on Cookie. Go get it Baby," Missionary Tisdale yelled. "Looks like somebody's forgot how to be proper," Carmen teased. "She's just got the fever," Nona said. "This is where

I run my best race," Cookie thought. Chin to knee. Bring the trail. Heike came with. Lane 3. Lane 5. Lane 4 - five meters ahead of the rest of the field. The three girls hugged and walked back to the finish line. Cookie looked at Lana, giving her an approving nod. "Ain't no shame in your game girl. You gave us a run for our money." "Speaking of Money," Heike said, "Keisha is getting ready to run. You go girl, bring home that money!," Heike encouraged as Keisha handed her sweats to Nia. "Time to get somewhere. I'll be back in 2 minutes and 15 seconds Nia." And she was – dispensing of the competition with the quickness – 2.14.13 to be exact. St. Julius placed second and third, with Morristown, a very tight fourth. Keisha immediately went to Coach Ashford claiming to have a stomach ache. "Okay, we'll put Latifah in the 4 x 400 in your place."

"Okay, Popeye, it's your turn." "I just hope your daughter can deal with the quickness of my Gazelle." "Panthers make meals of Gazelles, my brother." "Humming birds and alligators…" Etienne pulled 'Roni and Aiesha Brayboy away from the group for one final word of instruction. "Listen to me ladies. She (Saida) ran 11.61 in the relay – make her run the curve hard. If she stays with you, bury her in the next fifty yards before she can transition." "You want it, you got it," Aiesha said, then pointed at 'Roni. The two rubbed their noses and walked onto the track. "She is 'Poetry' – nice in the curve Popeye, but can she hold on down the back stretch?" "You just pray your daughter runs that 23 point you said she would." Carmen beat her husband's leg nervously. "This is your day Baby. Take us to Tennessee!" The Panthers went one/two once again – 'Roni, 23.4; Aiesha; 23.43, Saida, 23.6. Albany Metro finished fourth. "Sapp, you got one smooth daughter. You sure she's not part cheetah?" "She's been touched by an angel, good brother. An angel named Wilma Rudolph." Popeye laughed and shook Sapp's hand. "See you at the Nationals this summer!"

Cookie winked at Pooh before she backed into the blocks. "Remember girl, if you look good, I get good pictures." "Quiet from the infield!," warned the starter. "Two more events before the drama is over," Quinn told Pooh. "I hope it's over quick. I'm tired, hungry and ready to go home." "Girlfriend, you ain't said nathan.' My feet are killing me." Cookie was out first, in lane 5. The first four hurdles were uncontested. Then came the two Gazelles with Albany Metro in tow. Lanes 4, 6, and 7. The Gazelles finished one and two, 46.0 flat and 46.13. Cookie finished fourth. She hugged the girls as they walked back to the finish line. "It's all good. I got mine earlier." "True that girl," the Albany Metro runner said.

When 'Tonya came to Coach Ashford claiming to have a sore quadriceps muscle, she became suspicious. "What's going on, Keisha?" "You're asking the wrong sista, Coach." "Geordi, I smell a rat!" "Let's go with it Etienne. We can't force them to run. Sean and Latifah are fresh." "Alright

Girlfriend," Keisha encouraged. "You get a chance to get some get back. Break Napthali off a little sumthin' sumthin' and we (seniors) can all go home with a medal." Oops. The rat was exposed. Etienne and Geordi couldn't get mad. The girls were trying to share the wealth. State was a once-in-a-life-time thing. Why not let everyone have a part in their own destiny. The ritual performed, the new relay squad took to the track. "They flipped the script," Keisha sighed. And they (Springfield) had. Napthali was their lead off runner. They needed to get the lead quick in order to defend their title. "I hate it for Sean," Ciara said. "Tramaine still has to handle her business," Heike said. Last dance – last chance.

Napthali got out good in lane 2, running the curve with an effortless glide. She led the field at 200, much to Springfield's delight. Popeye could taste the victory already. If his Lady Grace brought the baton through the next 200 meters in the lead there should be "no catch." 54.2 seconds at the exchange. The Gazelles had a ten meter lead as the other teams serially broke for lane one. Albany Metro – 55.3; East Crenshaw – 55.9; Sean 56 flat – fourth position. "You go girl," and Latifah was off, her work cut out in front of her. The battle between Marshall High and East Crenshaw was nothing new. Fueled by enmity and desire, they flew through the first curve shoulder to shoulder. Springfield remained in sole possession of first place down the backside while Albany Metro was swept into the see-saw battle for second place. East Crenshaw surged with fifty meters left to run on the second leg, heel to toe ahead of Albany Metro and Marshall High.

Nervous electricity pulsed through the cluster of sprinters awaiting their chance to dazzle the crowd. The officials staged the girls according to the position their teammate held as they neared the exchange line. "Springfield, East Crenshaw. Albany Metro, Marshall High…" Amber felt the tension. However, the pressure of being in fourth place was relative. "One minute; forty-eight point-eight seconds. One fifty point-nine. One fifty-one. One fifty-one point one…" "You go girl!," the Marshall High contingent yelled collectively. "I hope Pooh gets this picture when Amber soups Crenshaw and Albany," Cookie said. "Ow! You didn't have to pinch me!," Heike screamed. "Oops!" "Go ahead Amber. Represent girl," Pooh snapped frantically. Once tried by fire, Amber saw gold. A 54-second split. "Ring-a-ling-a-ling!" The bell lap. There was virtual silence in the stadium as Amber bequeathed the baton to Tramaine. It was as if the two melted into one. No verbal command – just a nod as Amber hit her mark. Tramaine was in the wind. Phoenix. What had begun as a 2.3 second lead had been gnawed down to a 0.8 – second edge. Time elapsed - 2 minutes 44.3 seconds versus 2 minutes 45. 1. Fifty-three point eight seconds to victory.

One hundred – sixty – five meters to the tape. Tramaine remembered why she hated pyramids. 200M, 300M, 400M, 300M, 200M. Five successive 165's (meters). "Strength, endurance and speed!," reverberated through her mind. "It's now or never, Tramaine. Don't just go to the wall – KNOCK IT DOWN!!! Try as she may, the Gazelle couldn't hold the panther off. Strength and stealth prevailed. The air was suddenly darkened by a host of purple sweatshirts resembling a flock of vultures waiting to feast on carrion. Damon and Ramon didn't understand why their daddy was hugging 'that lady' and jumping up and down but they grabbed Mommy's hands and followed suit. "Hey Popeye," Sapp teased. "I bet you people in Springfield don't play bid whist, do you?" "Where you goin', Sapp?" "Fifty-four two. 54.6, 55.5, and 55 flat. Your coach played his Aces too early." "Napthali would say 'true dat'. My hat is off to your girls," Popeye gestured. Sapp and the old heads said, "Solid."

HOME AGAIN

'Roni and Tramaine shared front page billing in the Bradford Sentinel Sunday Edition. "LADY PANTHERS RUN VALIANTLY AT STATE CHAMPIONSHIPS." Story on page 3C. "Last Thursday, the Marshall High School Lady Panthers track team embarked upon a quest to surpass their feat of being named Regional Champions only a week ago. The mission – slay the dragon, defending State Champions Springfield Gazelles. Their domination of the sprints, half mile and relays doused the dragons' fire. However, it wasn't enough to vanquish the beast. Springfield's cumulative point totals in all events helped them to retain their title by a slim margin of two points. Coaches Etienne Ashford and Raimont (Geordi) Forney expressed their pride in the Lady Panthers and thanked the graduating seniors for anchoring such a great team. A perfect end to a near perfect season. REGIONAL CHAMPIONS AND STATE RUNNER-UP. WE CONGRATULATE YOU ALL."

The story Quinn wrote for the school paper was tempered with school spirit and camaraderie. "Of all the extra-curricular activities this school year, going to the State Girls Track and Field Championships has been the best. Team Captain, Veronica Sapp, brought home the gold in the 100 and 200 meter dashes. It is safe to say she is the fastest High School girl in the State. It is so apropos for an athlete to join the 'I'm all that', throng that I was taken aback when Keisha Money and LaTonya Walker feigned sickness, to allow Sean Hale and Latifah Battle an opportunity to play a direct part in the Panthers' victory. By forfeiting their positions on the 4x400 meter relay team and a chance for a second gold medal, their effacive gesture had the desired outcome in that every senior member of the track team came home with at least one gold medal. At least that is Coach Ashford's speculation. I thank the Principal, the coaches and especially the team for allowing me to be part of their swan-song. YOU GO GIRLS!" Quinn Apple, senior sports writer CLASS of 95.

Malik and Cookie were at McDonald's having lunch when they noticed Talley and Mare Tolg, another Majorette lieutenant. "I've still got to finish the choreography for the senior class play," Cookie said, suddenly reminded of her commitment. Malik was more interested in the school paper he'd brought along. "This article is tight, Cookie. Did 'Tonya and Keisha really lay it down like that?" "If I told you that Malik, I'd have to kill you." "You'd do your Boo like that?" "In a New York second!" "Well, I guess this inquiring mind doesn't need to know. I'm just glad you got yours." "One out of three chances. But it's all good, you still love me." "Excuse me," Talley interrupted. "Andrea, I hope you don't get angry with us…" "I might." "Page and I thought it was too much to ask you to concentrate on going to State and do the choreography for the class play so we asked Mare to help us while you were gone." "And?" "We want you to do the dance of the butterfly emerging from it's chrysalis near the end of the play – symbolizing graduation and maturity." Cookie looked at Mare and laughed. "Good looking out girl. I was sweatin' how I was going to keep my reputation in effect." "Think nothing of it. I wanted a piece of the pie too. From one dancing fool to another, break a leg. See you tonight at 6 O'clock."

Everyone arrived home to find an invitation to attend a pool party in Killian Forest. AT & T made mad money as the silver envelopes, emblazoned with a black stallion crest, gave rise to the collective cautious anticipation. Malik called Jacques, Malcolm and Kadeem. Malcolm called Foots. Foots called Pooh who was already on the phone with 'Tonya and 'Roni. Cookie called Heike and Chenelle. Heike went over to Mother Graham's so she could see what T.J. thought of the whole thing. "Damon must have bumped his head. I hope he doesn't think any body is going to come to his party after all the confusion he's caused this year!" "I don't know what the brother is up to, Bae Ruth. Maybe he wants to set it all right before we all graduate." "T.J., I know he was your boy back in the day, but…" "But in my heart of hearts, he's still my nig even if he has been trippin' since he moved to Killian Forest." As always, Mother Graham was listening from the wings. "You babies listen to your grandmother for a minute. There is always room to forgive. David was a man after God's heart and did some terrible things. Still, God forgave him when David confessed his wrong. You call the rest of those children and tell them to give that boy a chance. You don't know if or when you'll see each other again after you leave here in June. Call him up!" "Yes mam," the cousins answered. Then they made the phone calls. Everyone agreed – senior class play Friday night, Damon's pool party Saturday.

DAMON'S DAY

The pool party was scheduled to begin at 12:00 noon. Kadeem and Chenelle were the first to show up at 12:15 PM. Damon had called Kadeem and asked that he and Chenelle show early. They needed to talk before everything started jumping. Gamma answered the door, hugging them both. "Chenelle, you're still the prettiest of them all, baby." "Thank you, Gamma Edwards. This is Kadeem Betancourt." "How are you baby? I'm sorry you had to go through with my grandson. God only knows why we do what we do." "It's over now, Mam. I'm fine and so is my hand. Are you going to be swimming with us today?," Kadeem teased. I don't think so baby. This party is for you children." Kadeem wanted to ask where Judas was but Damon answered that question when he came into the foyer. "Don't worry, my brother. Judas is at the kennel for the weekend. I wanted you and Chenelle to come over first so I could apologize to you personally before I do it publicly. I don't want anyone to think I'm fronting. Everything I did and said was foul.

236

It took my pops finally getting in my chest to make me see how blessed I am. Anyway, Kadeem, I want you to know I give you much respect. I hate to admit it, but Chenelle is too much lady for me. I need to let go of yesterday and get into the real. You're the brother that's effect." "It's all good, Damon. I think we all learned something this year. Me, I still don't know everything but that's your history. I have to accept that. Chenelle has to be all that and then some for a brother like you to have gone this nut over," Kadeem said, pointing at his wrist. "Anyway," Chenelle said. "Cookie said she and Malik will be here around 1:00 PM." "Good, because I have some talk for them too."

Linford and Sharon greeted the rest of the kids as they began to filter in. "Girls, you can change in the second room at the top of the stairs if you need to." Thank you, Ms. Sharon," Pooh said. Cookie gathered the girls together asking if they were ready to get into the pool. She had a mission – a need to put an exclamation point on her chapter with Damon. "This is Damon's room. The place I learned the most important lesson of my young life. You gotta know who you are. Be true to you." "Preach girl,' 'Roni laughed. "Yea, make your daddy proud," 'Tonya added. "Y'all know you're wrong for that. A sista is lookin' out for her girls and you wanna jone. But I ain't got nothin' but love for ya," Cookie said, pretending to cry. "You are truly crazy, girl," Heike said. "We know what you're trying to say. We just hate it was you who went out like that." "Hey. Are we going to change into our bathing suits or talk about Cookie's bad day?" "Anyway!," Pooh said. There was little surprise when Chelsea and some of the other cheerleaders walked into the back yard. Page and Talley turned a few heads only because who'd have thought either of them would wear a pair of daisy-dukes. "Gimme a break people, this is a pool party, isn't it?," Talley said. "Yo, Page. Are you going to show…" "Okay, Andrea. We don't want to go there." The surprise was seeing Miss Bennett. Sure, she was Damon's babysitter when they were little but wasn't this pool party for students?

There were 50 meter races (two lengths of the pool). Relays. Chicken fights. Some played Charlotte's Web in the deep end and a few more demonstrated their breath control by having tea parties. After Brent scratched his back showing how close he could get to the board when doing a cut-a-way, Linford decided it was time to start serving the food. "Okay, we got dogs, hog, ribs, burgers and fish steaks. We've got baked potatoes, steamed corn, potato salad, coleslaw and a variety of soft drinks." "Mr. 'E', this is the bomb," Foots said. "It rocks for sure," Spawn said. "Thank you Eric and Mason but it was Damon's idea." Olivia got her food and started inside to talk to Gamma. However, before she got through the doorway, Cookie stopped her. "Miss Bennett, I know you're one of the down teachers and all, but I'm a little confused why you're the only one Damon invited?" "You'll find out before the day is over. The answer to your real question is: everything happens for a reason and I have mine. My name is truly Bennett and

I ain't in it. Are we here?" Cookie hugged Olivia and just looked at her thankfully. What's done is done.

MAKE IT PLAIN

Everyone had their fill of the smorgasbord the Edwards has spread and began to get restless. Sharon refused to let anyone get back into the pool until 6:00 PM. "You know you have to wait at lest one-half hour before getting into the water after eating." "Aw, Mrs. 'E'!" "Stop whining, Foots. You know she's right," Pooh teased. "Get him girl!" "Alright Heike, I'm going to tell Brent you got a thing for him." "Please, I like my coffee dark just like my momma." "Oooh, you're so bad," Keisha teased. Some of the football crew started gathering their things to leave. "Hold up everybody. I got a few things I want to say before you jet." "Make it plain, Demonseed. It's your party." "Looka here, knuckleheads, playas and Ladies; I need to apologize to everyone for all the foul things I've done leading all the way back to second grade. T.J., you know you been my nig since pampers almost." "It's all good, boy-e," T.J. said, pounding his fist to his chest and flashing Damon a peace sign. "To all you ballers, much love for you and good luck at the schools you got accepted to. I ain't mad at any of you – I dissed myself. You represent Marshall High proper because I'll be bringin' the noise from Clemson. Kadeem and Malik, you brothers got the best of the fab five. Mad props to you; I was a fool." "Don't play yourself like that, Damon. We know a brother makes mistakes, but we grow from them," Malik said. "True Dat," Kadeem agreed. Cookie and Chenelle looking at each other, laughed. They huddled the girls together and then waved Damon over. Damon never suspected their next move. They tackled him and started kissing him. "We hated you once, but we've loved you all along." Then they threw him into the pool.

Olivia, Sharon, and Gamma stood at the patio door laughing. Damon crawled out of the pool laughing just as hard. "Are you three going to let them do your son, grandson and brother like that?" "Stop!," Keisha hollered after the word "brother" settled on her ears. Everyone was just as awestruck. "That's right, I said brother. All these years I've wished for a sister, she was right under my nose. Many times at school she's told me I shouldn't diss women and girls like I do and I'd just tell her to talk to the hand. Finally, my pops had to serve me some humble pie before I accepted that this ain't my world – that and being dissed by the schools I wanted to play for. Keisha had to push her chagrin off on someone else. "See Heike, I told you he didn't hit it." "You know you wrong for that Keisha. It was you who said, 'he done hit everything else, he might as well try to get a teacher too." "Both of you need to quit," Chenelle warned. Cookie looked at Olivia and winked – now understanding why she was there for her. It must have been a trip to live so close to your family yet be so far apart. "Everything happens for a reason," she whispered.

ALMOST THERE

Mother Graham was basting the ham she planned to serve for Sunday dinner when T.J. and Heike came in. Heike cut right to the chase. "Grandmother, did you know Ms. Bennett was Damon's sister?" "Yes, Bae Ruth, I did." "Why didn't you tell it?" "Baby, I know you all think your grandmother is too nosy for her own good. You will learn as you grow older why things happen the way they do. Some business is nobody's business until who's ever business it is wants it to be known. That wasn't my business to tell, Bae Ruth. Now, do you have anything else you want to ask your nosy grandmother?" "I'm sorry I came at you like that, Gram. It's just that..." Mother Graham cut Heike off. "Remember, who's ever business it is will tell you when they want you to know." "I guess you're right. I learned some things while we were at state that could have only come from the horses' mouth. Gram..." "What's that boy's name you're going to the prom with? Have you decided what you're going to wear to the prom? I need to buy the material and get it to Nona."

243

"Okay Gram. I get the point. No more questions. His name is Jamal Diggs. I thought you wanted to make my dress?" "I do, Bae Ruth, but I know the rest of the girls are having their dresses done by Nona and I thought you might want that too." "Gram…" "It's okay child. Sister Henderson is quite the seamstress. You just promise Grandmother she can make your wedding gown." "Thank you Gram," Heike said. The hug and kiss she planted on Mother Graham's cheek left no doubt she understood the sacrifice her grandmother just made. She would go to the prom wearing a "NONA HENDERSON!" Who needs Versace and Armani.

The choir loft at Mason A.M.E. was the alternate meeting place for the girls when they couldn't make it to Davenport Bridge – especially on Sunday. Heike, Pooh and 'Roni sat on the lower pew while Chenelle, Cookie and 'Tonya on an upper one. "Girl, this has been a trip weekend. First Cookie shows out in the play. Then Damon's party was off the hook. I almost died last night when my grandmother said she didn't mind if your mother made my dress for the prom." "Who you tellin', sista. I was too through when my moms told me she asked her if she would do it." "All I can say girl is flow with it," 'Tonya interjected. "Say that again," Cookie said. "I'm going to be the show just like I was Friday." "Please," 'Roni said. "You know the only reason Chenelle was homecoming queen is because I wouldn't accept the nomination." "Ooooh, why you wanna go there, V-E-R-0-N-I-C-A," Chenelle laughed. "You know I'm clowning girl, but, I am going to be tight too." "I just know none of you'll look like anything if my moms don't do the dresses." "Why are you in there dippin' Kenny?" "Yea, disappear, squirt. This is WOMEN'S business. You need to go find Tangela and play little girl games," Cookie said. When Chenelle looked at her sternly she realized that was truly foul. After all, it was her who'd let a nobody shake her game. "I'm sorry, Kenny. I shouldn't have gone there." "It's all good. I shouldn't be in your business, either. 'Nel, Pops is ready to roll. Momma said she wants to get started on your dress as soon as we get home. Peace out." Then Kenny was gone. "You know your little bother always brings out the stupid in me, Chenelle." "You don't know!," 'Roni agreed. Chenelle had already forgotten about it. "See ya'll later."

"Daddy, have you seen my purple bunny?" "I was hoping you didn't ask me about that thing. I threw it out yesterday while you were at the pool party. Sade got a hold of it and drug it into the back yard. When I was picking up the shreds, I found this." He reached into his wallet and produced a Ramses condom. "I ain't the one, Daddy. I think you need to talk to Kenny." "Babygirl, I'm not blaming anybody. I just think it's time to be sure of things. I don't need to quote statistics about pregnancies and social diseases. Those things you know. In two weeks you'll be a high school graduate. I'm scared to death but I have to let you go and grow. Momma and I talked about this last night." "Daddy..." "Hear me out, Babygirl. We hope you will remain a virgin until you get married but we have to be real about this. College is going to open up a whole new world to you. We want you to be ready just in case you can't control the fire. Sororities - fraternities; just the freedom to be you. God forbid you get attacked. Get with your mother and make that appointment." "Okay Daddy. It's not what I want to do but if you and Momma will be happy, I'll do it." "I'm not saying you have to become sexually active, just be ready. You don't know who or what's on campus anymore." Chenelle went to her room and called Cookie. "I'm going to break Chelsea's @*!" "What's up, girlfriend?" Davenport Bridge, here we come.

"It wasn't enough for her to give my panties to Damon. No, the b@*#! had to put a condom in my bunny." "What?" "You heard me right. That…!" "Don't curse, Chenelle. That's my job," Cookie joked. "And you fussed at us when we kept bumping into her." "Yea, but my daddy wasn't sweatin me then. He thinks I should get on the pill before I go away to school." "And?," 'Roni said. "Remember I started the pill in the tenth grade?" "Yea, but that was to regulate your period. Not because you daddy thought you might start giving your stuff away!" "Wait until the prom to bust her up. That way you won't have to miss any school," 'Tonya said. "True dat – Finals and graduation are next week," 'Roni agreed. "Then it's all over," Pooh said. Her statement hit the gang like a ton of bricks. It was almost over. Grown. Suddenly, Chelsea's prank didn't carry as much drama. There was a strained pause, then Chenelle said, "It's time to go home. I need to call Damon."

"Don't lie to me, Damon. Did you know she put that thing in my bunny?" "We talked about it but she acted like she didn't go through with it after she brought me your underwear. I was through with it after the Christmas party. I know I acted like a Buster but I meant what I said at my party. I'm sorry. I'll talk to your pops if you want me to." "Save the drama, Damon. He doesn't know you had anything to do with this. Thanks for being honest." It's on.

FINISHING TOUCHES

"Nona, this is Red. I have Chenelle scheduled at 10:00 AM, Cookie at 11:00, 'Roni at Noon, 'Tonya at 1:00 PM, Heike at 2:00 and, of course, my baby is last. She wants to look like Jada Pinkett with that short haircut. Girl, I'm going to cry when I cut her hair." "We're going to be busy today, girl. I still have to put the lace on Heike's dress and the sequin trim around 'Roni's neck. You don't know how many times I've stuck myself this week girl. If I see another eye hook, button or zipper again it will be too soon." "I hear you girl. I promised Pooh I would personally do her nails even though that glue makes me nauseated. What a mother won't do to show her love." "But they've made it girl. They deserve this love – all six of them." "Jimmy (Mr. Hall) convinced two of his co-workers to chauffeur the kids around this evening. Carmen and Ramona are going to be busy tomorrow morning preparing breakfast for them when they finally decide to come in." "Victoria and Samuel want to pray over them before they get out there though." "I don't see anything wrong with that, girl. Lord knows those children are going to be crazy tonight. I gotta go Nona. My shop is calling me." "See you girl. Make sure you hide Pooh's camera so she'll take some time to enjoy herself." "Don't worry. When she's with Eric, her mind is gone."

Everybody met at the Tisdale's for prayer and pictures. Then Jimmy and his friends ushered the six couples to the limousines. The boys were cleaner than clean in their tuxedos. The girls dazzled in their "Nona's." Sequins. Strapless. Side slits. Lace. Tantalizing, yet modest. All personalized. All Darlings of Mason Street A.M.E. First stop, dinner at Zula's. Clam Chowder or Crab legs. Smoked Salmon or Halibut garnished with sliced almonds. Brown rice. Mixed vegetables or glazed carrots. Pineapple upside-down cake or chocolate mousse. "Miss Zula, your dinners are the bomb." "Thank you, baby. You all be careful tonight. It's the first night of the rest of your life." Kadeem handed her Walter's Visa Gold card and told her to take a $20.00 gratuity. "God bless you baby." On to the dance. The limousines pulled into the archway of the Sheraton as the valets took the keys of the students who'd driven themselves. Jimmy stood at the door helping each lady out as she emerged onto the scene. 'Roni and Malcolm were first, followed by Cookie and Malik, then Chenelle and Kadeem. Next came Heike and Jamal with 'Tonya and Jacques after them. Last but not least, Pooh and Foots. Jimmy kissed each of the girls' gloved hand in turn,

adding one to Pooh's forehead. "I'm so proud of you, Pooh."
"Thank you Daddy. I'm proud of you too." Redemption.

"This is how we do it," was pumping when they entered
the ballroom. "I saved you two tables even though you dissed
me and Nadia," T.J. teased Heike. "What are you talking
about, cousin?" "You could've invited us to ride in the limo
too!" "It wasn't personal T.J.," Pooh interjected. "My daddy
told me about it last night and told me to pick five more
couples so everybody could be comfortable." "I think we
could fit you in on the way to Kadeem's though," 'Roni said.
"Our moms are getting together and fixing breakfast in the
morning." "I'm with it. How 'bout it people?," Malik asked.
"Pooh, you have the last word," Kadeem said. "I don't think
my daddy would mind. I'll just let him know when they
come back to get us." "Cool for school," T.J. said. The next
song – "I ain't mad at ya'." Salt-n-Pepa, TLC, MC Lyte,
Immature, and the Boys II Men's "Sympin' Ain't Easy" got
everyone crunk up before the DJ slowed it down with Mariah
Carey's "Hero," Zhane's "Love Me Today," and finally – Janet
Jackson's "Again." Chyna and Mason were dancing next to
Cookie and Malik. What better time for Chyna to tell Cookie
of her plans for the evening. She decided to wait until the
end of the record so as not to spoil the mood. The DJ went
right into another Janet song, "That's The Way Love Goes,"
slightly more up tempo. Janet Jackson triple – "Because
of Love," got everyone crunk again. "Hey Andrea, that's a
pretty dress you're wearing. Can I talk to you for a minute?"

"You're working that mini-dress too, Chyna. What's up?" "I decided tonight would be the night I explore my possibilities. You know what they say about prom night." "Listen girl. You need to save that drama until you're truly ready. Trust me. You need to pay attention to all those billboards around town saying, "Virgin…it's not a dirty word." "But you were telling me it's about women being with men, a few months ago." "It is Chyna, but all things in their time, girlfriend." "It's my choice, Andrea." "Whatever. Just remember, 'no glove, no love,' okay? Don't make the same mistake I made!" Chyna looked at Cookie quizzically. "We don't need to go there, just do the right thing." "Okay!," Chyna agreed reluctantly.

"What was that all about?," Malik asked. "Oh, she was just complimenting my dress," Cookie said. 'Roni noticed Chelsea rushing to the bathroom - perfect timing for Chenelle to TALK to her. "Ladies' break." "Punch break," Malik announced as the girls left the table. Damon met the guys at the punch bowl. "You brothers got it going on - the limousines and all that; tight to death." "True that, Damon. We are 'bout it, 'bout it' tonight. You're pretty tight too. You pulled a senior," T.J. laughed. "You got down on that, my nig. Tiffany made her rules plain at my pool party. It's just a date for tonight." The boys were still laughing when the girls came out of the bathroom.

There had been drama in the bathroom, but not what they'd anticipated. Chelsea was already paying homage for her indiscretions when the girls caught up to her. Hyperemesis gravidarum. Missed menses. Chenelle smiled at her crew. Poetic justice. When the next slow record came on, Chenelle asked Kadeem if he minded if she danced with Damon. "No pressure. I'll dance with Tiffany." Damon didn't suspect Chenelle had an ulterior motive until she whispered, "I hope you and Chelsea aren't having the same problem you and Cookie had." "What?" "Do you know what it means when a woman gets sick for no apparent reason, my brother?" "Say what you mean, Chenelle!" "I hate it for you, Demonseed," Chenelle laughed as the record ended. "She never called me Demonseed before," Damon thought aloud. Then he figured out why Chenelle had been so cryptic. So sarcastic with her hope that he wasn't having another problem. It wouldn't be fair to Tiffany to talk to Chelsea now. He'd have to call her in the morning. Make the bed, you have to lie in it. Cookie shook her head when Chelsea returned to the ballroom. From enmity to empathy – bonding from similar dilemma.

"Nadia, call your peeps to make sure they're cool with you being out until tomorrow morning. Make sure they know we're going to end up at the Betancourt's." T.J. called his uncle to let him know he was leaving the car at the Sheraton. "Go 'head, young blood. I'll pick it up. I thought it was foul too that you and Heike weren't hangin' with the same crew tonight." "Good lookin' out, Uncle, but it wasn't Bae's bust. Pooh was thinkin' too fast when her daddy told her to pick some friends." The gang left the Sheraton enroute to "Jammin' 247 – The Groove Spot." They danced until 3:00 AM. Closing time. "Where to now, Pooh?" "Drive us along the river Daddy." "Anything for my Pooh and her friends." Jimmy motioned the driver on. Down the river. Across the bridge. Pass the ghost factories in East Crenshaw. They got out of the limos on the East Crenshaw side at Foots' request. He started walking toward the water with Pooh close behind. Turning to Pooh, he said, "take the boutonniere off for me, please." Telepathy. Everyone knew what he was to do. Like birds of a feather, they all took their corsages and boutonnieres off and flanked him. "To you, Uncle T.C. I'm sorry you never got to do what I'm doing now. Much love to you. May I be all those things you couldn't." Then he placed the flowers upon the water. Silently, everyone followed suit. After a few somber moments passed, Jacques broke into a lament. "I don't know about the rest of you but this brother is ready to eat two cows!" "You're about a knucklehead, Jacques. I 'preciate you though for keepin' me from getting too lost over my uncle; come on ya'll. Jacques is right on time. Thanks, Mr. Hall." "Solid." Old head and New Jack hugged each other. Off to the Betancourt's.

The girls took their heels off as soon as they got back into the limousines. The final signs of fatigue were setting in when they pulled into the circular driveway. Though not quite antebellum, the two chandeliers hanging from the cathedral ceiling graced the foyer with a historical ambiance. "Make yourselves at home," Ramona said as Kadeem led the gang into the family room. Everyone scrambled for the sofa and loveseat – except Chenelle. She strolled over to the platform in the bay window, fluffed the cushions and sat down. "Good morning, Zulu," she said, placing the fluffy, black tom cat in her lap. "I thought that was a stuffed animal," Nadia said. "That can be arranged," Kadeem said. "Watch yourself, K.D. You know he's your sisters' baby. Breakfast will be ready in ten minutes." Cookie, Pooh, Heike, Nadia and Chenelle succumbed to the cushions and warmth for the dual fireplace adjoining the family room and the breakfast nook. "Look at them," Ramona laughed. "The only reason 'Roni and 'Tonya are awake are these blueberry pancakes. 'Tonya makes it her business to be at my house for breakfast on Saturdays." "You know that's right, Miss Carmen." "So I guess it's going to be you two girls and seven guys," Ramona said. "More eats for me," Foots said to T.J. "No, my brother, I think you mean more for your feet."

The prom over, time to get on with the business of finals and graduation practice. For the majority of the 400 seniors, finals were mere formality. Rumor had it that the race for valedictorian and salutarian was so close the computer refused to tally up the two finalist GPA's. In the end, it would come down to the Physics finals extra credit points.

INVESTITURES/ BACCALAUREATE

P arents, invited guests and the junior class sat in the outer rows of the auditorium, anxiously awaiting the entrance of the class of '95. The next hour would usher in the changing of the guard – a new senior class. Tariq James, junior class president, sat on the dais beside Mr. Marksbury, beaming with pride. At precisely 11:00 AM, the brass quartet, comprised of graduating seniors, trumpeted the beginning of the ceremony.

"Ladies and Gentlemen, please welcome the graduation class of 1995." The procession of young men entered from the right and the young ladies from the left and filed into their seats in the middle of the auditorium. "Class of '95 be seated. Class of '96 and invited guests, you may be seated." Mr. Marksbury called to Kadeem to the stage to deliver his last speech as student body president. "It has been an honor to lead this student body over the last year. Our school's namesake was a champion of all the virtues I strive to live by...justice and equality for all." The audience sat captivated by his eloquence, inspired by his promise to continue in that vein. He nodded at Tariq, signaling his closing. "Tariq, I bequeath this gavel to you to lead the Panthers of '96 in the spirit of the late, great Thurgood Marshall – academically and socially. Raise the standard to the next level. Class of '95, thank you for being beside me, Peace!" Drama. Tariq accepted the gavel and moved to the podium. Taking the reigns, he made his first official motion.

"Ladies and Gentlemen, please stand while the senior members of the Panther Chorus lead us in the Alma Mater one last time." It was over. Mr. Marksbury directed everyone to remain standing as the class of '95 exited the auditorium. Keisha began to snap her fingers as the class of '95 filled the aisles. Like birds, the rest of the flock joined in - A syncopated stroll versus a march. The parents and guests followed the seniors of '95 out of the auditorium. Yvette Money couldn't get outside quick enough. "Keisha, you're a mess, girl." "You should'na ever told me you and your girls did the same thing when you graduated, Momma." "Yea, Yea, Yea," Yvette conceded.

"We graduate in just four days," Talley told Page. "Yea, it all seems so anti-climatic." "For you maybe, but for me, it means a trip to Spain before going to Villanova for freshmen orientation." "Is that your graduation present?" "Sort of.

Remember the money I made working at Pizza Hut? Well, my folks told me to use it to pay for my vacation. They were just trying to teach me to be responsible."

Inside, there was a different party. "Marshall High Class of '96, you may take your rightful places as Marshall High seniors," Mr. Marksbury announced. PANDEMONIUM. The center seats filled in a nano-second. "You may now turn your rings around so your crest is displayed prominently. Have fun getting 96 people to spin them. This assembly is over." Tariq started chanting, "Who you with?" "Ninety-six!" "Who you with?" "Ninety-six!"

FINALLY

Monday evening, 'Tonya received a phone call from Mr. Marksbury. So did Kadeem. "I am happy to announce that you'll be honored above the rest of the graduating class. Prepare a brief speech. Tomorrow night will be one for you to remember forever." Neither called either of their friends. That was Mr. Marksbury's last stipulation.

Tuesday morning found 'Tonya alone in Davenport Park with Chocolate Boy, her new Labrador pup, trying to entice her to play. "Go get it boy," she said, throwing the ball toward the bushes at the bend in the river. He came racing back with a sparkling blue pump instead of the tennis ball. "Okay boy, enough fetching for this morning. I gotta show this to Cookie." "Yea girl, that's the one Chyna was wearing at the prom."

The stadium was abuzz with the familiar Bradford chatter. The graduates stood beneath the bleachers. Anticipation. Twelve years of schooling would soon culminate in graduation.

"Chelsea, why haven't you answered my calls?" "There's nothing to talk about, Damon. You got what you wanted and so did I." Time for commencement. "Friends, family, alumni and graduates, I present Kadeem Betancourt, and LaTonya Walker - Salutarian and Valedictorian for the Class of 1995." Shocked, but not disappointed, Kadeem was brief with his remarks. 'Tonya on the other hand, couldn't mask her joy. "I often hear people say, 'dare to dream.' I dreamed of being an astronaut, not Valedictorian. I'm off to the Air Force Academy. To my parents and my girls, like Brandy, I don't know what I'd do without you,…you've always been there right beside me, my best friends. We always joke about 'what you gonna do when you get there?' I guess I'll have to get in where I fit in." In yet the last hour of their childhood, each of the teens would learn yet one more lesson – we never stop learning or growing. Issues must be resolved with expedience. Those which cannot be, we must accept and strive on – better or worse for the endeavor.

What you gonna do when you get there?
– Live and Learn!

ABOUT THE AUTHOR

I began writing as a fifth grader attending Patrick Elementary School. My father was stationed at Cape Canaveral, Florida.

My English teacher, a retired Air Force colonel, who was a stickler for proper grammar and penmanship, required us to write numerous essays and short stories every year. Additionally, we were tasked with putting together a book of poetry, from reknown poets, to present to our mothers on Mother's Day. Thusly, my appreciation for poetry and prose.

Upon entering the sixth grade, we learned how to spin a yarn and the use of "poetic license" - a skill honed by being "put on stage" and critiqued on our command of the audience.

The late 60's – early 70's, were a period of a social consciousness ignited by a rekindled pride of the people. Martin Luther King Jr., Malcolm X, The Last Poets, James

Brown, Goings, Van Peebles - The songs, movies, books and most profoundly, their speeches; charted the quest for the man I am today, David Elydge Vencil, aka, Dawud Nnamdi which means my beloved father is still alive.

I passionately write verse, tome, fact and fiction, that youth may become aware; and my generation can reminisce with a laugh and occasional cry. We have come so far with farther to go...

CPSIA information can be obtained
at www.ICGtesting.com
Printed in the USA
JSHW020823080622
26829JS00001B/4

9 781434 388476